Bede's

a novel by
Joe Stewart
www.bede-trilogy.weebly.com

edited by
Pam Stewart

Cover Photo of
St. Bede brought to Monkwearmouth
reproduced by kind permission of
Mgr. John Ryan at St Bede's Rotherham.
Design by Pendle Stained Glass

St. Paul's Jarrow
by
Jarrow Artist
Barry Hall

Forward

Welcome boys and girls (and any grown ups) and thank you for choosing to read my book about Bede of Jarrow. Some people call him Saint Bede but more about that later. This a fictional account of his life as a young boy growing up in the Kingdom of Northumbria, now Tyne and Wear. It is my idea of what could have happened to a young person growing up in a land where very few people could read and write and life was hard. Some of the things I have described could not possibly have happened, as the thing I have outlined had not been invented or discovered. This is known as an anachronism or something that is out of its time. An extreme example would be if I had Bede travelling in a car or an aeroplane.

I hope the anachronisms I have included are more subtle than that and you will need to read the book actively to see how many you can discover. Although some of my anachronisms are deliberate some will be accidental as, even though I was born less than a mile away from where Bede lived, I am ashamed at how little I knew about him before writing this book. I have tried to make this book interesting to both girls and boys. Girls have a prominent role in Bede's life. I hope that you enjoy reading about Bede and if you do, please look out for two other books in the series telling you about Bede as a teenager (Bede's World) and young man (Bede's Way).

I said earlier that Bede is known as a saint, which means he was a holy man who loved God. He is famous for translating the Bible, which is the most important holy book for Christians. In this book you will hear some of the stories from the Bible, which I think you may recognise, as the Bible has influenced the whole world for thousands of years.

I hope you will enjoy reading this book and I have used some vocabulary which you may not understand. Don't worry about this, just ask an adult or your teacher to help. Or even better still, look up the word yourself in a dictionary at home or in a library or online. I find that I remember the meaning of the word much better this way than by asking someone. Please write or email me and let me know the anachronisms you have discovered. I will try to reply especially if you discover some I did not mean.
Joe Stewart
October 2015
bedetrilogy@outlook.com
www.bede-trilogy.weebly.com
@bedethree

Contents

Chapter One

The heb Burn

On some original Roman maps of old Britain there are only three major settlements shown: London, York and Jarrow! This is the story of one inhabitant of the most inhospitable northerly outpost of the Roman Empire, who would soon astound the world and change the face of civilisation. It is my story and my name is Bede. I was born in a hamlet to the west of Jarrow, long after the Romans left Britain and my family own a small holding near a burn or stream called the Heb. From as early as I can remember, it was my job at the beginning of the day to bring water from the burn for the few animals we had and for my family.

I would take my time and bathe, when the weather was not too cold, in a rock pool I had made in the stream, near the confluence with the much bigger River Tyne. I had been warned by my family not to go near those dangerous waters because of the treacherous undercurrents but I must admit that I had often been tempted to practice my fishing skills in the river. I had frequently surprised and delighted my family by providing them with some small nondescript fish from the burn for their breakfast. But I longed to bring them the more substantial trout and salmon that, I had heard, sometimes populated the lower reaches of the river. However, for now they would have to make do with the odd offering I could muster, as I would need to persuade my father to come with me one day to catch bigger fish. He had promised to take me and show me the safe fishing areas when I was older but I don't think I can wait. I am a boy of twelve summers and my father says I must be a boy of thirteen summers before I can be allowed to fish the river on my own.

No matter how much I am tempted to cast my line in the Tyne waters of promise, I will not disobey my father. Although he is strict and has beaten me when I have been bad, I love my father. He has never beaten me for the sake of it, as some of my friends' fathers have. It has only been when his gentle correction has not worked or when my behaviour would lead me into danger. I know that any unauthorised fishing foray would fall under this category and that I would expect the worst. His gentle way has also been in evidence in his relationship with my mother. A fiery woman who always wants the best for her family, her natural exuberance often has to be tempered by my father's more conciliatory nature. Many a local dispute has been defused by my dad and, as such, he is held in high regard by his neighbours who often seek his advice and counsel.

I am the oldest (now) of five children and I have three sisters and a brother. Or I would have, if death had not taken two of them to the next world. Now I have no brother and two younger sisters and we all live with our mother and father in our three roomed house near the burn. Next to our house we have a small piece of land where we have two goats tethered and a pig snuffling on the remains of food and some scraps of peelings. We also own a donkey which father lends to our neighbours when they need it.

Using a bucket, I fill the trough with water from the burn and the animals stare back at me in unconcerned recognition. I then pour what is left into the flasks, made from gourds, which we will use for our drinking water, then stack the bucket next to our house. I can see thick black smoke streaming from the centre of the building which alerts me to my next task for the day. I must replenish the fuel needed to maintain the fire in the centre of house, which will burn continuously throughout the coming months of winter.

Prompted by the smoke I pick up the sharp axe, blade buried into a log near the entrance to our house. The blade is sufficiently secure into the log to prevent any curious neighbourly children from doing themselves a mischief but I am only recently strong enough to dislodge the tool, proving to my father that I am mature enough to be trusted with another chore. He had shown me the area beyond the clearing where I was to gather fuel. He had also shown me that, by carefully coppicing the wood, we would preserve our fuel and building materials long into the future. The future was not something we often thought about, as our existence was usually from long day to long day. The allotted chores would occupy me fully most of the day and there was little time for play with my friends. This usually took place after the second and last meal of the day which we would eat together.

I found the spot I had left off cutting yesterday and continued to lop off branches, then chopping them into smaller more manageable pieces, stopping only when I knew I had what I could manage to carry back. If more were needed, then I would return later in the day with my father, as it was imperative that the fire burned throughout the night. The fate of one of my siblings was testament to this necessity, having died of the cold one winter's night. It was my oldest sister Hilda who had that sad misfortune but my father has reassured us that her spirit lives on and that we will meet her again, along with our brother, who sadly died at birth. He often tells us stories of another world which we will go to after our death and of a being who will be a better father to us than him. We laugh at this fancifulness and tell him there is no better father than him. But we love these stories he tells us and, in that land between waking and sleeping, his words soothe us, as two realities merge.

He told us about some of the great men and women of Northumbria who had brought what he called the Gospel story to our land. This is the story of a special man, Jesus Christ, who would have a tremendous affect on the whole history of the world but I will tell you more about him later. One of the men who first brought the story to Northumbria was a man called Aidan who was a monk, which is a person who dedicates his life to God, who lived on Iona, an island in Scotland. He was one of the kindest and simplest monks there and he would have a tremendous influence on my father. One day the Abbot (the leader of the community) told him he was to go away from the island and go to the court of Oswald, King of Northumbria, to preach the Gospel to the Northumbrians.

Oswald was a Christian (a believer in Jesus Christ) who had been driven from the kingdom by the heathens, and while he was hiding from his enemies in Scotland he had visited Iona. Now that he was king, after defeating the heathen in a great battle, he wanted to make the whole kingdom Christian but one other monk had said that the English were unreachable and had no manners but Aidan thought differently.

"Perhaps you have been trying to teach them things that are too difficult. When you feed a baby you give it milk not meat. These people are like babies," said Aidan.

Aidan soon became a friend of King Oswald and told people about Jesus. They were especially kind to the poor and the King gave Aidan a small island called Lindisfarne off the coast of Northumberland, so that he could start a small community called a monastery where they all would live. The buildings were little more than sheds and the monks lived on milk, bread and vegetables with a little meat. Lindisfarne was a peaceful place but things were to change soon for Aidan and Oswald and my father would be lucky to escape with his very life.

Loaded with the wood for fuel I made my way back to our homestead nestling in front of me like a beacon of safety and security. I felt a warm glow and as I entered the confines of my abode I could just hear the sound of my mother's dulcet tones.

Chapter Two

Edwin

"Edwin....Edwin." my mother's voice resounded around the small compound where we lived and the two goats pricked up their ears in anticipation of some unscheduled feeding and then realising that this would not be fulfilled turned their attention to the few remaining tufts of grass at their feet. I have told you already that my mother is a woman not be trifled with and, on this occasion, her patience was reaching its limit. Finding that her invocation was not reciprocated by her spouse she turned her attention to me.

"Bede! Find you father for me at once. I need to talk to him before you leave."

As you may have gathered, Edwin is my father and I dashed off down to the burn in an obedient endeavour to find him. I have told you already that I love my dad (I love my mam too) and I especially love his name. He told me that he was named Edwin by the family who brought him up after he was orphaned as a baby, when his parents were killed in a Viking raid on his hamlet called Ford in north Northumberland. His foster family had miraculously found him still alive under a burning cart, with his mother and father slaughtered nearby. They had not known his real parents but kindly buried them before taking him with them further north. They then named him Edwin after the King of Northumbria and my dad often kidded us that he was the rightful king and that someday we would live in luxury in the city that bears his name; Edwinsburgh right in the north of the Kingdom.

My father's foster parents loved him but were quite old (about fifty five summers) and after his foster mother died his foster father, unable to look after him, gave him into the care of the monks on the Farne Island of Lindisfarne, a remote place off the coast. The island can only be reached by a damp sandy causeway which is covered twice a day by the tide. Many a poor person had attempted to outwit the cruel North Sea and paid for it with their life. Only the foolhardy would disregard the wise old monks who could judge precisely, after many years of study, the whims of the sea. Although only twelve summers old my father soon became expert in the ebb and flow of the waters. He was only a little older when Penda, the King of Mercia attacked and killed King Oswald at a bloody battle near Bamburgh. It looked as if he would march on to Lindisfarne and kill Aidan and my father would meet the same fate as his parents. However Penda could not take the strong castle at Bamburgh and so decided to burn it down. He piled up wood around it and when the wind was in the right direction he set fire to it. However, seeing the smoke from Lindisfarne my father told us how Aidan dropped to his knees and prayed to God to intervene. Immediately the fire turned towards Penda's army and Oswald's forces seized their opportunity and attacked Penda's men and drove them away. Oswald's brother was made king and Northumbria became safe from further attack.

As I approached the clearing near the burn I could see the diminutive outline of my father. This seemed strange to me as my father was a big man almost six feet tall. I quickly realised the reason for my father's unusually small height was that he was kneeling with his eyes closed and arms outstretched. I crouched behind a hawthorn bush and waited. I remembered my father telling me how special Lindisfarne was and how he had been schooled, first by Aidan and then later by Cuthbert. He was taught to be able to decipher symbols painted on parchment and then later to paint symbols himself. These symbols had meaning to those who were able to understand them and my father called this reading and writing; a skill my dad was passing on to me but which I find very difficult to do.

It was on Lindisfarne that my father also learnt to do what I was now witnessing. On the parchment which Aidan and Cuthbert had written were stories about a being who had first created the world and the animals and indeed us. This being had then entrusted this creation to us to look after for him, this being Aidan and Cuthbert called - God. It was in their house on Lindisfarne that they first tried to communicate with God as a community and this communication they called prayer. This was what my father was now doing and I knew it was important to him and what made Edwin my dad and I did not want to disturb him, no matter how imperative my mother's command. My dilemma was resolved by my father's sense of being watched and he opened his eyes and instinctively smiled in loving recognition.

"Bede my boy. Are you looking for me?" My father intimated to me that he knew what my purpose was and putting his arm around my shoulder escorted me back to our home. "Your mother is looking for me no doubt. Let us find out what's bothering her today." A knowing glint appeared in his eyes and I am sure I detected a slight raising of the eyebrows. As we approached our home, my mother caught sight of her errant husband.

"Edwin! Where in the world have you been?" and before he could offer any form of explanation she offered her own, "You know I don't hold with all that nonsense you go on about. Talking to who? God! You are filling Bede's head with it too I'll warrant." My mother, Hilda, was a down to earth sort of woman, the kind of woman who holds families together but not the type of woman you would want to get on the wrong side of.

"Hilda" my father's voice was soft with love and in seconds melted mother's heart and in that one word he was able to convey to his spouse the depth and the importance of what he had been doing.

My mother's face flushed scarlet and apologetically she told him how worried she was about the journey he was about to make and how little preparation he had made for it. He was quickly able to reassure her that he had made arrangements with our neighbours to look after her, the family and the livestock whilst he was away for four weeks or so. I was puzzled, listening to his detailed explanation of the arrangements, why I was not involved in these plans until he revealed, to the utter shock and amazement of my mother, that I too would be joining him on this momentous journey.

*　　*　　*　　*

It was now three hours since my father had made his announcement and my mother had not uttered a single word, although we were left in no doubt about her feelings by the cacophony of pans on wood. The day was growing dark and my father knew that he would have to broach the subject as we sat down to our meal.

"Hilda" This time the loving opener that had proved so successful a few hours ago was not going to work. This was just the invitation my mother needed.

"You know how I feel about that place. It's dangerous, the raids are getting more frequent. You of all people should know the dangers after what happened to your parents." The place she was referring to was Lindisfarne, the island where my father had been brought up. Some raiders from a far off land over the sea had landed on the island and there were rumours that these were just scouting raids and an invasion was being planned. The monks on the island had been so worried about impending raids that they had moved the body of their late Abbot Cuthbert, one hundred miles south to the cathedral at Durham. I have seen his resting place in this vast building and have thought that you would have to be a great man to be buried there. Little did I know that one day I would be lying at the opposite end of the building to this great man.

"Not all Vikings are unfriendly, look at that family near Monkton. Bede plays with the boy and they are good people." It wasn't what my father said but the way he said it that seemed to work and I could feel my mother's attitude changing. "You know I need to return to Lindisfarne. We all need me to return and it will be good for the boy. It is time he helped me and it will be good for him to see where I grew up." Every year, and sometimes more frequently, my father returned to Lindisfarne to work on the monastery the monks were building. In return he would get some provisions, usually piglets which we would fatten, and grain which would help us through the winter. But another and more important reason was a spiritual return to his roots. My father loved to feel the serenity and peacefulness of the island. My father called it a pilgrimage.

We all began to eat and my father continued to reassure my mother and, seeing he was having some success, he interspersed his reassurances with stories and jokes, till the whole family were laughing and even mother looked pacified. My sister Bridget climbed up on to my father's knee and begged him to tell us one of his stories he had learnt from Aidan when he was a boy. After much argument between the children, as to which tale was most appropriate, it was agreed that it would be the story of David and Goliath that he would relate. This was a particular favourite of mine as I identified with David a lot. He was a shepherd as a young boy but was chosen from all his brothers to be King of Israel. When he was looking after his sheep he would use his sling shot to protect them from predators. He had killed a bear and a lion. At night David would gather his sheep into a pen and he would actually sleep across the door of the sheep pen to ensure nothing could harm them. Dad told us about how he was asked to take some food to his brothers who were fighting the Philistines who had a huge champion called Goliath. All the Jewish soldiers were scared of him and would not meet his challenge. They looked in disbelief and ridicule at this skinny boy who boastfully said,

"I'll go, I have killed a bear and a lion, I'm not frightened," said Dad, putting on a high pitched voice that was supposed to be that of a boy. His voices were what we especially liked about his stories and they always brought them to life. But I told him that I was a boy, like David, but I didn't talk like that. Dad smiled and ignoring my protestations he continued the story. Unbelievably they agreed to let David have a go and brought out some armour to protect him. It was so heavy David kept falling over! So, after rejecting the armour which was too heavy for him, David carefully chose some smooth stones and loaded the best of them into his faithful sling shot.

"Ha ha ha, you are sending a boy to do a man's job. Come boy and let Goliath see you." boomed father using his hands to demonstrate the giant's power. He then told us how David, after loading his sling shot with a stone, swung it several times around his head. Goliath, bent double with his hands on hips in laughter, mocked the lad. "Ha ha ha, now you want to play games with me boy." Taking aim David released one side of the sling and out flew the stone. The stone embedded itself in the forehead of Goliath who stood rigid in surprise. As if in slow motion the Philistine fell to the ground with a shudder. When father reaches this point it is our cue to sum up the story and in unison we interrupt father.

"And David runs over to Goliath, draws his sword and....cuts off his head!"

Father laughs raucously and claps his hands in self congratulatory delight at his children's enjoyment of the re-telling. Bridget holds her ears in her hands in mock horror. We implored father to tell us more stories and, although he would have been agreeable, mother knew that this was a usual ploy by us to avoid going to bed.

"No more, children. Time for bed. There's plenty of work to be done tomorrow if these two are leaving us for a while and we will all need our rest." Father smiled lovingly at his wife, thankful at her reluctant agreement to entrust her beloved son to his care. Edwin knew that he would need the help of one who had entrusted His beloved son to a woman's care. Making his excuses he left us and I knew he was finding a quiet place to pray.

Chapter Three

kickbladder

I have a few days before I travel with my father to Lindisfarne and I hope to have some time to myself to play with my friends. One of our favourite games is kickbladder, which I play with lots of them. When dad returns from Lindisfarne he usually brings two or three piglets which we fatten up then slaughter and they feed our family (and a few of Dad's friends) over the winter. I don't like having to kill the pigs as we grow so attached to them but they do taste nice! We use every bit of the pig, even the ears which are quite crunchy.

Dad lets us have the pig's bladder which he blows ups; we couldn't do it ourselves, as it would make us feel sick. The bladder then bounces up and down when you throw it or kick it. When we go down to the nearby village we put two sticks in the ground, eight paces apart, at each end of the field. We divide all our of friends into two groups, which we call teams, usually four in each team, and we try to kick the pig's bladder between the two sticks, which each team defends. The winner is the team which kicks the bladder through the sticks more times. I don't know who invented the game but my dad used to play when he was young but it was not as popular as it is today and it is played right throughout Northumbria.

I have two special friends who I always have on my team. One is called Joseph, who is an excellent kickbladder player and he is my cousin. His mam, Veronica, and my mam are sisters and we have been brought up more like brothers as we are the same age. My other friend is Odin. His dad is a Viking from the land over the seas. Many people are frightened of the Vikings and are worried about an invasion. However, as my dad says, not all Vikings are bad and Odin's dad and my dad are friends. Odin's mam and dad sailed over the sea when he was just a baby to escape from a cruel overlord. They were soon accepted into our community and Odin's mam and dad want to become Christians like my dad. My dad has been teaching the three of us to read and write. Joseph is the best at this but Odin and I struggle. Today though, all thoughts of study are put to one side as we plan our game.

I am going to call this morning on Odin and Joseph, who live on the lane leading to Monkton Village. We play on the field near the village, as it is one of the few areas which is not being used for crops or animals and is flat enough to play on. There we will meet the rest of our friends and then pick our teams. Most of the time the three of us play together on one team but today Odin has been chosen on the opposite side. The match kicks off and soon Joseph and I are working well together and we are two goals up and are well on top. I cross the bladder for our teammate Caedmon to score a third goal. The other team are in disarray and most of them are picking on Odin and blaming him for their situation.

The game stops, as two of the opposition players are arguing with Odin. I say arguing but they are really yelling at him and they are joined by Caedmon, who although our player, is also the older brother of Eldrick who is the main critic of Odin. These two brothers are often the source of trouble when we play. My mother says Caedmon is a bully but dad says we have to make allowances for them, as their parents died when they were very young and they are now being brought by an aunt. As ever the dispute gets around to Odin's ancestry.

"Look Viking boy, we have lived here longer than you so why don't you and your family get back in the boat and push off back to Viking land?" said Caedmon, weighing in with all the authority of an older and wiser sibling.

I could see Odin flushing with anger, as any reference to his Scandinavian roots brings a mixture of pride and shame which he can only express by the use of his fists. He was near the point of full expression when I decided to intervene.

"Hey come on lads its only a game. Look Caedmon, he's only half your size mate," I said in a half jocular fashion nodding towards Odin.

"Aw I see. You think I should pick on somebody my own size?" he replied threateningly, adjusting his body and moving into my own personal space. I remembered my mother's advice to stand up to bullies as they often back down. I remembered too dad's plea to make allowances. Then I recalled some of the conquests of Caedmon I'd heard about. I drew myself up to my full height, which enabled me to look him squarely in the eye. I tried not to let fear betray me in my voice, as I calmly advised him:

"No that's not what I am saying. I just think that if we all calm down we can resolve this without any violence."

Caedmon was biting his bottom lip, looking like a volcano about to erupt when a deep young male voice broke the tension.

"Boys! Boys! Kickbladder lovely! OK Joseph..... on me head!"

"This ain't finished holy boy." Caedmon brushed past me and sat on the bank awaiting the outcome of the dialogue with our new visitor, namely brother Godric from nearby St Paul's Monastery. Joseph, Odin and I met with him every week at the monastery for reading and writing lessons. This was a favour to my dad and Odin's dad for the work they did for the monks. Father has asked if my sister Gertrude can join us, as he believes girls should be educated too. My mother doesn't agree though.

Joseph duly crossed the bladder which Godric despatched with his head into the empty goal. He punched the air with childlike delight then gathered the boys round him to give them some interesting news.

"Glad to see you practising lads. Some great news. Around Pentecost there is going to be a kickbladder tournament for many teams in the area and we want you lot to represent St Paul's, although you are going to have to come up with a name for your team. The competition is going to take place at the old Roman fort of Arbeia at South Shields. There's just a couple of things though."

Simultaneously the boys looked elated and crestfallen, as they anticipated some insurmountable obstacles to this great and momentous news.

"First of all there must be at least eleven players on the field at anyone time but you can have more, so you can swap them around." The boys looked at each other, as if telepathically agreeing that this would not be too difficult to address. The cleric continued, "At least four players in each team must be.." He paused, "...girls!"

The young monk was met with a wall of deafening silence!

"Oh and one final thing. You must have an adult to look after things, to kind of manage what you are doing and organise you." Thankfully we all thought that Odin's dad, Tor, would agree to do it, as he had experience of a similar game they used to play in his homeland.

Caedmon and his brother glared across at Odin at this latest news and the party of boys broke up with them going their separate ways murmuring to each other, the only audible word being - girls! Caedmon flashed a parting glance at me, as if to say that there was unfinished business between us. I and my two friends walked with Godric.

"I know you are off to Lindisfarne soon Bede but you will be back well before Easter and Pentecost is well after that, so you'll have plenty time to practise. I couldn't help but notice an atmosphere when I arrived. Is everything OK?"

There was a subliminal question in Godric's apparent concern as he had just been teaching us about Lent, Easter and Pentecost and I determined not to let it go unrecognised.

"Yeah, just the usual. Caedmon and his brother picking on young Odin. And oh, that'll give us a good fifty days after Easter to get our team tactics right"

"You know what the good Lord would say to you about Caedmon?" asked Godric.

"I know, I know - turn the other cheek," I replied.

Godric smiled in satisfaction of a job well done, both in church tradition and Gospel teaching. Bowing, he waved and took the lower track back to the monastery.

The trouble is, I thought, that if I turned the other cheek then Caedmon would take full advantage with one of his legendary right hooks! I had to think of a way to diffuse the situation and following my discussions with Godric, the kickbladder tournament was just the thing.

Chapter Four

At the Well

It is the day before we are due to leave for Lindisfarne and dad tells me he has some good news for me. We walk out to a special place which only I and dad know about. It is a small gush of water from the ground which flows out over some black and grey rocks. The water flow is well hidden from prying eyes and far from any track or path. When I asked dad how he found it, he just smiled and said an angel showed him.

"Here son, taste some of this water." He gently lets the water caress his fingers and I cup my hands and scoop an ample amount into my mouth and let it dribble down my chin and on to my tunic. It tastes so pure and I feel it instantly refresh every part of my body. I close my eyes and take a second single handful. "You know Bede, water is so important to give us and our animals life and is used a lot in the Bible. Jesus calls himself "living water" and that anyone who drinks the living water will never be thirsty again. Water was used to baptise, as it is a sign of making people clean, not only from dirt but from sin."

"You have been baptised dad, haven't you? I think I would like to be baptised too. Is that what your good news is, am I going to be baptised?"

"No not yet son, no it's not that. It's about the journey tomorrow. I thought it's not good for you to be stuck with me and some old monks for four weeks. So I have had words with Joseph and Odin's mams and dads and they have agreed to let them come too. Mind you they will have to do their fair share of work and of course their families will get some of the produce I will receive from the monks."

"Wow that's great dad. Thanks, I mean that...well that really means a lot." I had wondered how I was going to tell the lads I wouldn't be around for the kickbladder training.

"I'm not sure you will be quite so happy with my other news. Your sister Gertrude is coming too, as I think it is time she was included in your activities. We'll spend a night at your aunt and uncle's place at Alnmouth before pushing on to Bamburgh, a night there at the church and then on to Lindisfarne. We will have to camp out somewhere up the coast on the first two nights, so that'll make four nights and five days to make the journey."

The news about my pain of a sister travelling was more than compensated for by the news of the lads coming and breaking the journey at Aunt Agnes and Uncle Aelred's place. Aelred's was my mam's younger brother who had done well for himself, after leaving Jarrow five summers ago. He now had quite a large holding of land and grew wheat and barley and had numerous cows, pigs and sheep. We would be adding to the monks produce on our return journey.

"You will have to break it to the lads that they will have do quite a lot of walking. Your sister can ride on the cart but the beast is not strong enough to carry all four of you."

The beast in question was Parsley our family's young ass, which was more a pet than a useful member of our tribe. This was the first year she would be called upon to bare the burden of duty. In the past my dad had rented a donkey from the big farm at Mill Lane but, after doing some work there, he accepted payment by means of a brown foal with a distinctive black cross upon its back. Dad told us that the cross on the back of the donkey is a sign from God because of the importance of the animal in Jesus' life. Mary, his mother, rode on a donkey to Bethlehem, where Jesus was born. Donkeys were present when Jesus was born in the stable because there was no room for them in the inn. Then Jesus Himself rode triumphantly on a donkey on Palm Sunday, with all the people waving and cheering. Donkeys indeed have played a big role in the life of Jesus.

"That's okay dad! It'll help us all get us fit for the kickbladder tournament," I said.

"Aye Godric told me about it. But I gather you've had a bit of bother with Caedmon and Eldrick picking on young Odin. They're sad those two you know. I think they are jealous because he's got what they haven't - a mam and dad. Because he's a bit different, those blond Nordic looks, he's an easy target for them. I'm glad you stuck up for him but I don't want you getting into a fight with Caedmon," said dad. I could tell from his tone of concern that he did not expect that I would emerge victorious from such an encounter.

"Well I took on board your advice about making allowances for them and I think I may well have changed Caedmon's whole outlook on life," I replied with an air of confidence.

My father looked intrigued by my rather extreme claim and urged me to explain in more detail. I told him about a meeting I had with Caedmon on the way home from the kickbladder match. Having said goodbye to my friends I was alarmed to see him further down the track, apparently waiting for me. Before he could threaten or intimidate me, I grabbed the initiative and told him how pleased to see him I was, because I had an idea which I was sure he would like.

This totally disarmed him and I sat down next to him to explain. I told him that, if the team was going to be much bigger than the four a side teams we've been playing in, then we would need a different approach. Eleven players would need a player on the field who could organise them and tell them what to do; a leader like the captain on a ship. A captain on the field. That player would not only have to be a good player but someone with the authority to unite all different sorts of other players. Caedmon was hooked, nodding furiously in agreement.

I also told him that I thought that he was the person to do the job and that I would put my idea to the other players when we next met. Caedmon flushed with embarrassed pride. However, I said that it would mean supporting the whole team, even those he did not particularly like. He knew I was referring to Odin and looking me full in the eyes, like our earlier encounter, promised he would treat all players fairly and equally. We agreed that he would repeat this promise at the team meeting and, shaking hands, we went our separate ways amicably.

"Well done son. I knew you would solve the problem somehow. You have that air of calmness about you that makes people want to be in your presence. They feel safe and secure. It's a great gift son, well done. Well I'll have to get back or your mam will skin me. Are you coming? I might need that air of calmness," said dad smiling at the thought of the encounter, yet to come, with his wife.

"Not yet dad. I'll just stay here a few more minutes. I think this is where I get my calmness from. I love this place it is so peaceful," I replied.

My father agreed and bade me farewell. I sat near the water gush and bathed my face with the pure liquid. Holding my visage up to the warm late winter, early spring sun to dry, I closed my eyes and prayed for the success and safety of the forthcoming journey we were about to make. Although I was excited I was also a little anxious, it being the first time I had left the confines of the Heb Burn, Jarrow or South Shields.

After several minutes I become aware of a beneficent presence nearby. I blinked against the watery sunshine and was just able to discern the outline of a tall person, standing no more than ten metres away. I say person because as my eyes focused I could not distinguish if it was male or female. Strangely I also felt as if I knew him or her, which I suppose explains why I was so untroubled about the meeting.

"Greetings Bede. Do not be afraid. I have a message for your father. Tell him it is time. Tell him to bring you here at Pentecost. Don't worry, he will know what I mean."

I experienced no fear or trouble at this request and in fact felt as if the mysterious stranger had my best interests at heart. I had no means of explaining this sense of ease but I knew that I should make some attempt at showing the stranger that I would concur with his wishes.

As I tried to murmur my agreement I felt my eyelids slowly close and must have awakened only a matter of seconds later, to total solitude. Unsure whether what had occurred was a dream or reality, I returned home with the whole episode slipping totally from my consciousness, to be replaced by thoughts of scoring the winning goal in our kickbladder tournament. This was the reality now, this was my priority and, as any young boy would, I put all thoughts of this encounter behind me.

Chapter Five
Girls, Girls, Girls

Unsure about the validity of what had happened earlier in the day I decided to keep my own council, finish off my chores and slip away for one final kickbladder training session before leaving for Lindisfarne the following morning. It was a fine spring evening and the sun still had some warmth in its rays and I was excited by the prospect of a kick around with my mates before the hard work of the forthcoming journey. I skipped down the track, lined by yellow daffodils and blue crocus. On the way I met a few of my friends and told them about my idea of appointing Caedmon as captain, which was met with universal approval. However the good news was tempered by Odin telling us his dad was too busy to manage our team. This did little to endear Odin to the rest of the lads but I understood what the demands were on Tor's time.

All the lads turned up buoyed up by the thought of preparing for, and winning, the forthcoming kickbladder competition but our anticipation was not matched this evening by our skill. I don't know quite what it was but we were all over the place with our game. Misplaced passes and missed open goals were common and there was a noticeable lack of team spirit, with little niggling arguments breaking out all over the pitch. I awaited for the inevitable argument to break out.

However I was pleased to see that Caedmon was taking his new role of captain seriously. Once or twice he intervened as Eldrick sought to make Odin the scapegoat for our poor form. After about an hour of trying to string a few passes together we gave up and congregated in the centre of the field to take on some water. Two jugs were passed round the teammates and we alternately slurped from the terracotta containers. Feeling the responsibility of his captaincy role, Caedmon was the first to break the silence.

"We'll have to play a lot better than that if we want to win the competition," he said, tempering his criticism with just a little air of encouragement. He obviously realised that as captain he now had a duty not to be so negative and in recognition of this he continued, " I suppose we will have plenty of time to get things right when you lot get back from Lindisfarne." I nodded in agreement and drank deeply from the earthen container, glugging down the crystal cool liquid. It was Odin though who voiced a reply.

"I'm sorry lads I seem to be off my game today." he bowed His head in contrition, taking upon his shoulders the blame for all our woes like an oxen bearing the burden of the heavy yoke. His long thin blonde hair blew across his face and he gently brushed the flaxen tresses from his eyes. Eldrick puffed out his chest and cleared his throat, clearly a prelude to a prolonged diatribe of faults against the youngster. Before he could give vent to his criticism his brother interrupted with more analysis of the day's play.

"It's not your fault Odin, it's not you, we were all poor today. It's just one of those things. Some days it feels as if we have never played together before. The other thing that is bothering me is this rule about girls. Where are we going to get our hands on some girls?"

We all fell about laughing at Caedmon's statement. Only he failed to realise that he sounded like some desperate old man looking for female company. It didn't help either that his own brother seemed to be the one that was enjoying his faux pas the most. He flashed him a withering look which brought both Eldrick and the rest of us back to our position of paying attention to our wise leader. He continued,

"Look! Am I the only one taking this competition seriously? If we don't improve our attitude we are going to get stuffed by the other teams. At the moment we don't have a clue!"

"He's right!" The comment of agreement came from a disembodied voice which did not belong to a member of our group. Moreover the voice was unfamiliar and....noticeably that of a women. We scrunched our eyes in protection against the lowering sunlight and focused in to see the outline of a tall, slim and elegant lady. She introduced herself. "Hello, my name is Agatha, I live in Primrose and I have watched you playing when I have been passing on my way to the village. I have been impressed. You are all quite good but you lack organisation and I am sure I could help you to improve." She had a presence about her that lent an authenticity to her words.

We all sat motionless, transfixed by her beauty with our mouths hanging open. Gradually her words permeated into our minds and the ridiculous thought of a women having any notion of how to play kickbladder began to take shape. Amongst her many attributes you can add mind reading as she continued,

"I know you must thinking that I can not know anything about your game but I assure you that I do know about organisation and that if you let me help you, then you will notice a difference in your play. There is one other thing I can help with too. I have two daughters who also play kickbladder, so I do know something about the game. Not only that but they have two friends who also play. In fact they could give you lot a decent game."

"I don't think so." smiled Caedmon and he glanced at the rest of us in attempt to get our agreement. We all stood up and drew ourselves up to our full height. "We've been playing together for a while now. And with respect I don't really think a....girl can really understand the complexities of the game." He shook his head in a profound and sage way, determined to convey the depth of his knowledge and his standing as our leader.

Wow, we all thought, did Caedmon really just use the word complexities? He really is taking his new role seriously and our admiration for him began to grow. I felt pleased with myself for having thought of the idea of making him our captain and, despite how we were playing, his new role was a success. However he was now about to receive a challenge from the stranger that was going to be difficult to refuse.

"Well" replied Agatha, "give me a few minutes to bring the girls over and we will have a short game. I'm sure you'll be convinced," She smiled at us with her hands on her hips assuming that our agreement was a mere formality.

She had called our bluff and we had no option but to agree. As she disappeared over the hill, Caedmon implored us all to do our best as he didn't want to be beaten by 'a bunch of girls.' Within fifteen minutes she had returned with a motley crew of four girls varying in height. We gazed at them dumbfounded as they stood, also with their hands on hips, as Agatha introduced us to Jane, Helen, Mary and Teresa. We agreed a ten minute game of boys versus girls and they said they did not mind that we had one extra 'man.' As we lined up to start the game Agatha seemed to be lost in discussions with her team of girls and then spent time making them stretch and warm up. We stood in wonderment and waited for them to line up against us.

We had kick off and immediately Joseph jinked his way into a shooting position and a cross shot into the corner saw us a goal up. He wheeled away from the goal putting his tunic over his head in glee, as the rest of us mobbed him. I think we overdid the celebration and were soon made to pay for it as the girls deftly passed their way to three goals!

A further two soon followed and we found breath difficult to come by, as we wheezed our way to the end of the short game, keeping the damage down to five goals. We had never felt so humiliated, being beaten by a bunch of girls!

We gasped out our excuses but Agatha brushed them aside, telling us that the girls were not better than us but it was just a matter of organisation and preparation. Heads hung low we had no option but to agree to Agatha's plan to be our organiser.

She said she knew of one more girl and two boys which would bring our team up to eleven with a couple of reserves. If she could organise us as well as she had the girls, then we told ourselves that we would have an excellent chance in the forthcoming tournament.

As three of us were setting off for Lindisfarne the very next day, a training plan was arranged for our return. She gave us some limbering up exercises to do whilst we were away and we all returned to our respective homes, chastened by our defeat.

We indeed had lots of food for thought.

Chapter Six

The Journey

The black sky was torn with jagged strips of white and the outline of a crescent moon could still be detected, even though the bells from St Paul's Monastery had struck the hour five times. The late February air evidenced the coldness of the early morning through the smoke like breath of two figures, struggling with each other for dominance. The former was my father, impatiently trying to fit a bit and bridle on to the novice animal. The latter a mule stubbornly and successfully resisting.

"Bede! Bede! Please come quickly and help before I......"

My dad wasn't normally such an impatient man but he obviously had a lot to contend with today and so I obediently ran to comply with his request. I held Parsley's head between my hands and immediately she calmed down. I stroked her head gently with alternate hands all the while making reassuring noises. This enabled my dad first to prise open Parsley's mouth and slip in the bit, then he dextrously slipped the bridle over her head as we gracefully changed hands with each other.

"Thanks son. I told you...the gift, the gift. I would have been here all day and still not got that on, without your help," he said with a sigh.

I smiled and continued to help dad as we harnessed the cart that would carry our little bits of luggage and my sister on the outward journey and, hopefully, would be laden with produce on our return. We were soon joined by Joseph and his parents and Odin and his dad Tor and his mam Freyja. Having loaded their even smaller luggage, we just awaited sister Gertrude who was getting her final instructions from mam. I was only a toddler when my aunt and uncle moved to Alnmouth and Gertrude had not yet been born. My dad had promised them, on his previous solo meeting, that he would bring both of us on his next visit. Mother marshalled her daughter as she prepared to give her the benefit of her guidance.

"Now then young lady remember your manners and be sure you make a good impression. Make sure you help your aunt and uncle round the house and look after your dad and the boys on Lindisfarne. Oh I wish I was coming with you." Gertrude sighed at mother's instructions having heard them so many times before.

"Yes mam I will. Perhaps I can tell them you will see them next time," she replied shrugging her shoulders impatiently.

Dad interrupted the dialogue, explaining that we would need to be at the jetty at Tyne Dock within the hour to take advantage of low tide, when the crossing would be less hazardous. He embraced mother as well as the boys' parents and we eventually set off as the church bells struck again, this time adding one further strike to the former five. We were all in an adventurous mood as we sang hymns that we had learnt from Godric but adjusting the volume whenever we approached any homestead so as not to awaken the sleeping residents.

Before too long we were at the jetty, awaiting our first major obstacle. Tyne Dock was chosen as the safest crossing point on the river because of the natural slipways on both banks which allowed donkeys and carts to board a simple flat barge like craft. This then was towed across the river by a large row boat, sculled by two brawny ferrymen. All the children were to be transported in the row boat with the ferrymen and Dad was to stand guard with the donkey and cart on the somewhat exposed barge. However I pleaded with him to allow me to help, as I could pacify Parsley if she became spooked, and reluctantly he agreed as he was convinced by my argument that we were crossing the river at the safest low tide period. Nevertheless we both knew that the crossing was possibly the most hazardous part of the journey.

After settling the animal onto the barge and the children in the row boat, we embarked from the south bank, gliding effortlessly into the middle of the river. There was a strong bracing breeze in the offing, blowing from the North Sea, removing any remaining vestiges of sleep. As we approached the north bank harbour, the mother boat had to make a sharp turn to the left, resulting in an opposite and compounding effect on the barge which swung almost ninety degrees to the right. My father immediately inserted a handily placed oar into the water to arrest the turn and hopefully reverse its direction. Unsettled by the suddenness of both manoeuvres, the donkey lost its footing, instinctively kicking out with its right hind leg. Unfortunately this was to be in my direction and as my balance was even less reliable than the mule's, I found myself catapulted into the Tyne, a good fifty yards from shore.

Thankfully the Tyne is a clean river and the first few gulps of water had no adverse effect on me. However I realised that any further uncontrolled consumption would result in my drowning and I determined to fight to keep my head above the water. It was on the second or third surfacing that I heard my father's reassuring words.

"Remember the psalm Bed," he said. "When you walk through the waters I'll be with you, you will never sink beneath the waves."

A hairy arm was thrust into the water which I grasped as hard as I could and felt the comforting power of my dad's strength haul me to safety. As I lay gasping for air, I thought I detected a tear in his eye but it may have been the spray from the river. The children were glad to see I was well and, when we disembarked, my wet clothing was exchanged for a warm comforting blanket and dad insisted I ride on the cart with Gertrude. She ministered to my every need until we reached our night stop without further incident.

Our first evening was to be an overnight bivouac in a cave my father knew further up the coast, about a mile inland from the sea. Father set us all to gathering wood and soon a fire was roaring near the cave's entrance which not only warmed us but also roasted some rabbit meat brought from home.

We all ate as much as we wanted, supplemented by mam's bread and sat around watching Odin whittling away at some unused firewood. The outline of an animal's head could be seen emerging. My dad smiled in admiration and broke into our meaningless conversations with:

"That boy has got the patience of Job."

We laughed at dad and wondered who on earth Job was. Dad said he would tell us the story if we all promised to settle down afterwards. Assenting he began in his own inimitable style, using amusing voices to denote each character. The story of Job is to be found in the Old Testament of the Bible and apparently he was a good and just man who worshipped God. God loved him so much that he bragged about him to the devil, who said that he could get him to curse God. God agreed to let him tempt Job but he told the devil he could not harm him. We all booed whenever dad mentioned the devil and this added to the theatre of the story.

We were all saddened at the next part of the tale, when we heard that, whatever could go wrong went wrong for Job and he lost everything. House, possessions and family were taken from him and he was left to sit in dust and ashes. Even his wife told him to curse God and die! But he didn't! Three friends came and instead of helping him as good friends should, just added to his troubles, telling him it must be his fault that he is in a pickle. He must have done something to deserve it. Job realised that these were no friends at all. Then a young man who had heard of his plight came to see him and instead of criticising him began to tell him about the goodness of God. You see, in all his misery Job had lost sight of God and, instead of people telling him how no good he was, he needed someone to tell him how loving, forgiving, powerful and just, God is.

Then God Himself speaks directly to Job. He doesn't give Job any explanation of his situation but he asks if Job was there when He made the world, when He set the stars in place, when He set the boundaries for the sea? We were all sitting there awestruck as dad dramatically waved his arms to show the limitlessness of the sky and the rippling waves of the sea. We all cheered with gusto when we heard that Job repented and asked God for forgiveness, for not trusting in him. God forgives Job and gives him back more than he had before; houses, money and family. We all said what a strange story and wondered what could it mean. Dad knew that this was a ploy to delay bedtime, nevertheless he wasn't going to miss an opportunity to explain his story.

"Well boys...." then looking at Gertrude. "and girl. The story tells us that whatever happens to us we must never lose sight of God and His greatness. The young man is a Jesus figure, who always points the way to God. As friends we must be like him and not the three so called 'comforters' who could only criticise. Job probably wanted to know why all this happened to him but God does not give him any answer to his unspoken question. Sometimes there are no answers or no answers we would be happy with. Only trust! Trust in God! When Job did so then things changed for the better. It also tells that the devil is a beaten angel. Although he was allowed some power by God, it was only enough to hang himself. He demonstrates he is a loser - again. But we are on the winning side - every time. Now come on you horrible lot, you promised me. Bed time!"

Despite all our protestations and requests for more stories, we knew that a promise was a promise and after dad led us in a night prayer we all settled down to sleep.

Rising with the dawn chorus, we breakfasted on bread and cheese and hitching the cart we were soon underway again. The morning was frosty but dad said he liked it that way, as it made the ground hard under foot and easier for the cart. As the temperature rose only a little, the ground held firm for most of the day. Dad feared heavy rain as this would make life difficult for Parsley, not to mention for us foot travellers. The day passed uneventfully and the initial excitement had now waned and Joseph could be heard several times, asking if we were nearly there yet. The red glow of dusk was warming the sky as we made camp for the second night. This time a warming broth, using the remnants of the previous nights rabbit, prepared us for a night huddled together under the stars. Dad had a veritable blaze going, to stave off the cold and, unknown to us as we slept, he fed the conflagration, punctuated by fitful sleep of his own.

Day three followed the same routine, broken only by several impromptu meetings with fellow travellers. The journey was taking its toll on us children and as we ascended our final hill in the late afternoon twilight, we were bolstered by the sight of the warming and inviting lights of my aunt and uncle's homestead.

Chapter Seven

Alnmouth

Hearing the noise of the cart and the excited voices of five hungry travellers, uncle Aelred opened the door and broke into a broad smile and threw his arms into the air in recognition. Soon those arms were embracing first dad, then me and Gertrude. He expressed joy and surprise at the growth we had both achieved and, noticing two more additional potential family members, introductions were made to Joseph and Odin.

"Welcome, welcome everyone. You all must be so tired and hungry. Please come in but first you must hear our good news. Agnes!"

Before he could explain Agnes appeared framed by the door and, even from the travellers' front perspective, it was possible to discern the rounded shape of her belly, hidden under a thick green tunic. Her face was radiant and shone scarlet in the gloaming.

"You see brother Edwin, I am with child," said Aunt Agnes.

"I see that you are so blessed my child and your sister will be so happy for you both." Although Edwin and Agnes were brother and sister in law, his more advanced years allowed him to use the more fatherly epithet of child.

Edwin and Hilda also knew that their kin had long awaited this news. Father added, "God has truly visited His people. When is the baby due?"

Aelred motioned that we all should come in and informed the assembled group that it would, hopefully, arrive in three months time. Invitations and informal arrangements were made as to proposed visits between the families in the future and meanwhile Agnes was managing to prepare a meal, whilst at the same time agreeing or suggesting alternative arrangements to the ones proffered. Dad remembered we had not seen to Parsley, so uncle showed us where she would stay overnight after we had unhitched and fed her. The two men entrusted the job to us boys and strode back into the house, arm in arm talking about old times. Gertrude meanwhile automatically assisted her aunt in the meal preparation and before long we were about to tuck into a sumptuous feast of beef and parsnip and turnip, reflecting our uncle and aunt's new found prosperity. My uncle stood and quietened us with the motion of his arms.

"It is a great day for us to be blessed with the company of family and friends. Please God, shortly after Pentecost we will be further blessed with an addition to our family. We will return to Jarrow and Heb Burn shortly before the birth so that she or he can be called a true Tynesider. And Edwin, we would like you and Hilda to be godparents." holding his wife's hand he continued, "We can think of no better people to help look after our child's spiritual welfare. Please would you lead us in the grace." With that he sat down and tenderly kissed his wife's hand. My father's chair noisily grated against the Northumberland stone floor as he stood and began.

"Lord! I will say again that you have truly visited your people and blessed them with this new life. We ask for your care and protection on mother and child, as we remember how you cared for your own mother when you blessed her womb. We thank you for this meal which Agnes has so lovingly prepared for us and which Aelred has so generously provided for us, from your bounty oh Lord. We make this prayer in the name of our Lord Jesus Christ."

The grace was met with a hearty amen and we needed no second invitation to begin our repast. At the end of the meal, the three of us boys were deputed to wash the dishes and once completed we all huddled round the vast stone fireplace where an inferno warmed us. We marvelled at uncle's fireplace which was not in the centre of the room but formed part of the east stone wall. The smoke from the fire did not billow around the room like ours but was carried up the inside of the wall and out of the building through the roof. Dad shook his head from side to side in wonderment at such an invention. All four children found an ally in uncle, in our strategy of trying to postpone bedtime by calling for stories. Feeling truly ganged up upon by the whole group, with the exception of aunt Agnes, dad pretended to reluctantly agree and as we had heard about the arrival of a baby, he thought that this should also be the subject of his story. But, he inquired of his attentive audience, could anyone guess who this story about a baby was about?

Gertrude was bursting with excitement as she waved her hand and cried in her sweet voice.

"I know! I know! It's about Jesus! How he was born in a stable in Bethlehem and about his mam and dad. How the shepherds came to see him. And oh yes the three kings. Am I right, am I right dad?"

Before dad could answer, Joseph replied on his behalf,

"Well there's no need for your dad to tell us. You've just told us the story."

Everyone laughed at the matter of fact way Joseph interjected and Gertrude flushed with embarrassment at being the centre of attention. Dad now saw his opportunity to begin the unfolding of his tale.

"Well you're not too far away my daughter, as it does concern someone who is part of Jesus' family. I do though need someone's help in telling my story." Dad winked in my direction and I knew I would have to discharge the role of narrator in one of his epic productions, when he would use rhyme and numerous voices and accents to enhance the performance. I would be the straight man, whilst he garnered all the laughs from his captive throng. He mouthed the subject of the story and I understood what my role was to be.

So, I stood and began by telling them that this was a story about an aunt and uncle (the children ooed and aahed towards their hosts) namely Jesus' aunt and uncle called Elizabeth and Zechariah. He worked in the Jewish church called the temple. Elizabeth and her husband longed for a child but they were both quite old and, even though they had prayed to God, it looked like it would never happen. Then when Zechariah is cleaning the temple one day:

"All of sudden there was a bang and a crash
And there stood before him was angel Gabriel in a flash"

Then dad comes in as both Zechariah and Gabriel, you'll have to imagine the the different voices.

(GABRIEL)
"I bring you news that you must hear
And treasure it up in your heart so dear
It is word that will give you both great joy
Your wife will bare you a baby boy."

(ZECHARIAH)
"I'm sorry I'm old and my hearings not good
I think that I may have misunderstood."

(GABRIEL)
"The lad will grow up to make men and women think
But be careful he must not touch any strong drink
Remember what I say and then when I am gone
Explain to Elizabeth that you must call the boy John."

(ZECHARIAH)

"I think you must have got the wrong bloke

You see me and the missus are old - is this a joke?"

(GABRIEL)

"Zechariah! I am Gabriel I stand before God

I assure you that this plan has been given the nod.

But because you are so willing to doubt

Until John is born you will say nowt!"

Dad now mimes Zechariah being struck dumb, much to the amusement of the other three children; I've heard it all before, but it is funny the way he does it. The story goes on apace with friends saying there is nobody in the family called John. When Zechariah calls for a writing tablet and insists by writing on it - his name is John - then his speech returns and everyone celebrates. Dad concludes as John's dad by saying.

(ZECHARIAH)

"Thanks be to God I can speak again

My son will be the leader of men.

My story should be a warning to us all

You should never doubt the Good Lord's call."

Reverting to prose speech dad tells us how the boy John grew up to be John the Baptist who was responsible for turning many people away from their sins and towards God. Dad theatrically bows to all four walls to applause from one and all and then insists that I also take a bow too. There are cries of 'more more' but aunt Agnes is insistent it is bedtime and, in due respect to her condition and our plentiful supper, we offer no resistance. We drift off to sleep as she sings the Lord's Prayer to us.

"Our Father, who art in heaven, hallowed be thy name,

hallowed be they name

Thy kingdom come thy will be done, hallowed be thy name,

hallowed be thy name

Upon the earth as it is in heaven, hallowed be thy name,

hallowed be thy name

Give us this day our daily bread. hallowed be thy name,

hallowed be thy name

And forgive us our trespasses, hallowed be thy name,

hallowed be thy name

As we forgive those who trespass against us,

hallowed be thy name, hallowed be thy name

And lead us not into temptation, hallowed be thy name,

hallowed be thy name

But deliver us from all evil amen"

We all joined in the 'hallowed be thy name, hallowed be thy name' bits, but we were asleep by the amen.

The next morning, before breakfast, all the children waded across the River Aln to Cuthbert Island where the great man himself used to pray before he moved to Inner Farne Island. We played chasey and hide and seek before we heard our uncle's voice calling us for breakfast.

After a hearty meal we said our goodbyes and set out for Bamburgh, our last stop before heading over the causeway to Lindisfarne or Holy Island, as it was now being called by many people.

An uneventful journey, punctuated with running games of tag and songs along the way, culminated in our walking the final miles in absolute silent awe as the outline of Bamburgh Castle loomed into view. It was a magnificent sight and made us realise that its occupant must be a most powerful man who had defended his people from the Scottish and from occasional Viking raids. We all held King Oswald in high regard and dad was fiercely loyal to him.

Dad had been given permission for us to bed down in the small wooden chapel in the village and after eating a packed supper, prepared for us by our aunt and uncle, we settled down quickly to our beds. Dad had told us that we would need our rest as we would have to be up early next day in order to cross when the tide was out. This would leave a safe, dry causeway to traverse. We talked on into the dark of the night, telling eerie tales of ghosts and ghouls. until the candle flame lapped low as it drowned in the melting wax and extinguished itself. We slept soundly.

Chapter Eight

Lindisfarne

Dawn broke over the Northumberland coastline and the ass, silhouetted against the horizon, breathed dragon like breath into the chilly spring morning air. She shook her head against the bridle being held by Joseph, who gently stroked the animal in order to calm her. We waited on father's instruction to proceed, watching the wooden stakes which traced the safe causeway from the mainland to the remote island, acting as beacons to the wary travellers. To stray from the confines of these indicators would certainly be asking for trouble.

"Right boys and girl," bellowed my father, with sufficient volume to awaken the dear departed. "The sand should be just firm enough to take the cart. Gertrude you can stay on for the crossing but when we come home it'll be too heavy, with all the goodies we'll hopefully get. And for goodness sake stay inside the stakes. I don't want anyone sucked under." This only served to further confirm our fears and we took our first tentative steps across the damp strand.

We had heard numerous stories about people trying to beat the tide and had either been sucked into the treacherous wet sand or drowned. Half way across there stood, a good ten feet above us, a safe haven for those who had been caught by the tide. They would have to scramble up a rickety ladder to a square platform. However there would be little or no room for animals or belongings. We were determined that we were not going to be in that number.

Nevertheless the vision of the island shrouded in mist with the hint of the day ahead, was a humbling experience and spoke to that innermost part of your soul. I now knew what father meant about this place and how it was an integral part of his being.

We carefully negotiated the crossing and arrived safely on the island, which consisted of a partially built abbey and several small dwellings, or cells as the monks called them. Each cell was sufficient for only one person to live in and the abbey consisted of a church for worship and a communal hall, where the monks would meet together for meals. My father told me this was called a refectory.

We were met by a young brother called Gregory who took us to meet the Abbot, who is the head of the community, called Peter. Abbot Peter had been born in the border lands of Scotland near a town called Melrose. He had been a soldier but after seeing a vision on the very night that Aidan, the founder of Lindisfarne, had died, he became a monk and eventually ended up in charge of the community at Lindisfarne. He greeted my father like a long lost brother and was then introduced to all the group, beginning with Gertrude then Joseph and Odin and ending with me.

"Bede, Bede " he repeated, "my son I have heard so much about you. I have a feeling you are destined to be a great man. Have faith in God my son and listen to His voice. I know He has great plans in store for you." Then realising he had not included the others he continued, "As He has for you too my children. You must always pray and, as Mary said in the Bible, do whatever Jesus says. He will reveal His will to you, all you have to do is believe. Now then, Gregory will show you where you are staying. Settle in and we will all meet for lunch in the refectory. Just listen for the bell."

We were shown to a cell which was to be shared by the three boys. A bunk bed and a single were crammed into the small building. Father and Gertrude were to have a cell each. These cells were set aside for guests. We unpacked what little belongings we had and father gave us permission to explore the island, reminding us to listen out for the bell which would herald the call to lunch for us and the rest of the community.

We ran with a greater freedom than every before and the fresh air of the Northumbrian island refreshed every bone and sinew of our bodies. The sky was an endless blue and, although now March, the orange disk in one corner gave off some warmth. Or perhaps we are too young to feel the chill of the breeze from the North Sea. We climbed to the top of the sand dunes rolling down the other side, our bodies crashing into each other. The sand from the collisions, finding its way into every crevice of our clothes. Gertrude invariably found herself bringing up the rear and, losing her breath, she began to cry. This was often her first response to our teasing and it was always difficult to gauge the severity of her feelings. Odin and I ran on, making mocking noises but Joseph stopped and, seeing that she was in some distress, turned and offered her words of comfort. This made us both feel guilty and sheepishly we returned and offered our apologies.

"I'm going to tell dad on you Bede" threatened Gertrude. "Mr. blooming goody two shoes. I'll tell him what you did, leaving me like that." Then, after a long enough interval to get me worried, she began to laugh and I knew we were okay again. The idyllic silence, interrupted only by the sweetest of birdsong, was broken by the echoing metallic resonance of the abbey bell calling us to lunch.

We were all ushered into a great hall with a long table running horizontally across the hall, with two more slightly shorter tables running at right angles to the main table. We sat at one of these tables and nine monks processed into the room, followed by my father, then the Abbot. Most of the monks sat at the upper table with Gregory joining us. We all stood whilst the Abbot said grace before meals and we all sat down in silence. Two more monks came in one bearing two dishes of meat, whilst the other climbed some steps to a dais and began reading from the Bible.

Apparently this is common practice at mealtimes in monasteries and we heard a story from the Old Testament about Abraham. He was a great man of God and he had been promised by God that he would be the father of a great nation. His name was changed by God from Abram to Abraham. He was told that his descendants would be as numerous as the stars but there was only one problem; his wife Sarah could not have children and they were both growing old. One day three mysterious strangers came by and told Abraham that this time next year he would be a dad. Sarah was listening secretly and began to laugh in disbelief. The three men asked Sarah why she was laughing and she replied that she was now too old to have children, it just was not possible. The men told her that, nothing was impossible for God and said that when the baby was born that they should call the him Isaac, which means laughter.

As the meal of meat and vegetables, including carrots and cabbage, was served to us we gulped down the food, whilst listening to the story. We washed it down with a speciality of the monks, mead, which is a drink made from honey and wine. We could have only a little, as it is alcoholic and too much would make us drunk so some water had been added to it. The mead had been chilled and the cool liquid refreshed us as the story continued.

We were all very pleased for Abraham and Sarah but were horrified by the next part of the story. When Isaac was still a young boy, God spoke to Abraham and asked him to sacrifice his only son. Abraham was sad but, believing in God, he could only trust that everything would be alright in the end. It was quiet common in those days for people to sacrifice animals and even humans were sacrificed to their false gods but Abraham had never expected God to ask this of him. Although Abraham didn't realise it at the time, God was testing his faith and would make it clear to him that it is not sacrifice He wants but a humble and obedient heart. Abraham was being prepared for an important role.

So Abraham obeyed and got everything ready for the sacrifice and he and Isaac set out for the hill on which it was to take place. The boy was tied down and must have been so scared when his father raised his knife above his head to kill him. Just in the nick of time, an angel appeared and ordered him to stop! He told Abraham to sacrifice a ram that had got its horns caught in a bush. Abraham released Isaac and did as he was told.

When we heard that Isaac was safe we all let out a cheer of joyful relief. My dad tried to wave to us to be quiet, conscious of our holy surroundings, but the Abbot overruled him saying,

"No, no Edwin let the children be. They should be excited at God's word. Now children what do you think this strange story is all about then?" This was more of a rhetorical question, as he did not give us a chance to reply and so continued, "Why! God is showing us how much He loves us and how much He cares for us. God is telling us the He is going to sacrifice His own Son but, unlike Abraham and his son Isaac, God's son will die. Do you all know the name of His Son?"

Realising that this question was not of the rhetorical kind we replied in unison, "Jesus!!!"

"Well done and God sacrificed His only son for us, for our sins. You see, sin matters to God my children, not because it hurts Him but because it hurts us. All the sickness, death and evil in the world is caused by sin. But don't worry children because Jesus has overcome the world and sin, through His death on the cross. We must come to that cross and discover what Jesus has done for us personally. Like Abraham we must be girls and boys and men and women of faith. We must seek out God's will for our lives and obey His will, even though it might seem strange to us."

We stared at Father Abbot not knowing if we were meant to say anything in response but our predicament was resolved when he dismissed us with, "Now children off you go and explore this beautiful and special island," he said, smiling with a sense of satisfaction at being able to preach the Gospel, albeit to a captive audience. It gave him a sense of renewal at seeing such youthful exuberance and sparked memories of his own childhood, spent in a small village on the west coast of Scotland. It was through the preaching of Columba that he had first become a Christian as a young man. He subsequently helped establish monasteries in his homeland before being invited to become Abbot of Lindisfarne. Although he loved his vocation he felt the weight of his predecessors Aidan and Cuthbert on his shoulders. He welcomed the temporary relief of this responsibility and waved his assent to the children.

Glad to be released, we diligently obeyed the Abbot and discovered secret bays and beaches of this truly idyllic island. We met again later in the day for a further meal, this time taken in complete silence. The monks then met in the church for Compline, the final service of the day, when they would say their night prayers. Our father told us all to get a good night's rest as we would all be required to assist the work needed in this small community, which after all, was the reason for our long journey. Usually we took this as our prompt to have high jinks before settling down, however the Holy Island air had taken its effect on us and we found ourselves fast asleep in no time.

The following days were a delightful mixture of both work and play, assisting our father in the morning by fetching and carrying materials, and then playing in the afternoon. Odin however proved more skilful than the rest of us. Whereas we were mere beasts of burden, he was able to exhibit quite a high level of carpentry and was able to make small seats and window frames, a skill his own father, Tor, had taught him. It was fascinating to watch him mitring the corners of the frames, with a precise forty five degree angle, so that they joined perfectly. Father grew quite close to him and unselfishly passed on his own skills to him, however he ensured that he enjoyed his afternoon free time.

We paddled rather than bathed in the North Sea, although the vivid blue water looked inviting, its icy chill had a bite as severe as any vicious dog you could imagine. From time to time Gregory would join us when he had been released from his duties and would show us the secret harbours of the island. He showed us the best places to catch fish and, although we thought we were quite skilled fishermen, he was able to give us many tips to improve our techniques. Our most lucrative catch were crabs, which we caught off the makeshift main harbour and we were glad that we were able to provide some food for the table and help pay for our stay on the island, as well as justifying our afternoon free time. We were governed at all times by the sound of the bell tolled, by one of the monks, and which summoned us to meals as well as the monks to their prayer services. It was rung intermittently six times with three second intervals. We were also informed that the bell had an additional, if seldom used, function. It acted as an alarm call and if required would be rung rapidly until everyone had responded and had assembled outside of the church.

After a few days hard work, father produced something that made us all jump for joy. He said he had kept it back until now, to ensure that he got some work from us and as a reward for that work. It was a newly blown up kickbladder. We screamed in delight as he booted it over our head and across to a large cropped area of grass. We had all faithfully been doing our limbering exercises given to us by Agatha but to have a kickbladder to practise with, made us extremely happy. Gregory, although new to the sport, proved to be an excellent goalkeeper and even our Gertrude got into the game. Joseph, as usual was our star player, displaying excellent control and passing skills. He was never selfish though and always brought other people into the game through his accurate passing. He had a particularly good relationship with Odin, teeing up many goals for him through his assists, as he called them. Odin would head or volley the kickbladder into the goal without a moments hesitation. It was as if they had a sixth sense and were able to communicate with each other telepathically.

We sat one afternoon, after a hard morning's work followed by an energetic game of kickbladder, drinking cool crystal clear water looking out across the harbour. Gregory had an hour off himself and had been playing kickbladder with us. He nodded across the harbour to a point in the distance.

"See that island over there?" he nodded again until we showed some recognition. "That's Inner Farne, the island where Aidan used to live on, in order to be quiet and be alone with God and where Abbot Cuthbert went to pray sometimes too. Aidan was an Irish monk who spread the Gospel throughout the towns and villages of Northumbria. Although they never met, Aidan was a great influence on Cuthbert and they both loved the Farne Islands. It is a beautiful peaceful place." Gregory looked wistfully as if he wished he was there too. "Would you like to go? I could take you, if Edwin and the Abbot agreed."

We looked from one to another. None of us had ever been on the open sea before and the crossing of the River Tyne and been harrowing enough. But, not wanting to appear cowardly, we all agreed that it would be a good idea. However, when the subject was broached with father after dinner, he seemed reluctant to let us go. He was very conscious of his responsibility to our friends' parents. He would often tell us that he was *in loco parentis*. *This* is Latin for 'in place of parents' and father took this duty of surrogate parenthood most seriously

"I am not against the idea as such," he explained, "I have been there myself and it is a tranquil, peaceful place but I have responsibility for you all and none of you have been on the open sea before and none of you can swim." Father's fears were well grounded but Gregory explained that, if we were brave enough to master the icy North Sea, then he could teach us to swim in one of the safe harbours around the island and that we would only attempt the journey if the weather was agreeable. We were having an unusually warm springtime and I think that this persuaded father to agree to this course of action.

So, following our mornings of hard work, afternoons consisted of an hour or so playing kickbladder, then an hour cooling down in a shallow rock pool which was deep enough to enable us to learn to swim, assisted by an enthusiastic Gregory. We learnt first of all breaststroke, then front crawl. He taught us to tread water which enabled us to remain in one spot in the water. This would be helpful if we were unfortunate enough to fall overboard, as it would make it easier for us to be rescued. Finally we learnt how to float, then swim on our backs. This is a way of using less energy and helping you to survive for longer in the water.

After a week, we were all deemed competent enough to attempt a swim in the sea. The rock pool had been positively boiling in comparison with the North Sea and we all agreed that we would take no risks when in the boat, as the icy waters would be the last place that we would want to find ourselves. Gregory declared us skilled enough to attempt the journey and it was agreed that this would take place the following Sunday, after the Eucharist service. We would take a picnic lunch and spend a few hours on the island and father agreed, on condition that he too could accompany us. This would be a welcome day off for him, as he had been working ever so hard since arriving on the island.

Chapter Nine

Inner Farne

The Gospel reading at the Sunday Eucharist, prior to our departure, was particularly apt. It was Brother Gregory who read from the huge leather bound book of Gospels. From where I was in the church I could just make out the beautiful coloured lettering introducing the reading from the Gospel of Mark. The Lindisfarne Gospels where renowned throughout Northumbria and, according to my father, throughout the civilised the world, for their ornate illuminated accounts of the life of Jesus read at out at services in church. The Eucharist (coming from the Greek word meaning thanksgiving) is the special service where we recall the night before Jesus died when he celebrated the Passover Meal with his twelve closest followers, known as the apostles. He took bread and broke it and said, "This is my body" and wine and said, "This is my blood." This is a most sacred time for Christians and the Word of God is always read before these holy words of Jesus are used once again. Gregory drew himself up to his full height and, looking at those assembled, introduced the reading.

"A reading from the Gospel according to Saint Mark." he intoned, waiting for the congregation to settle down and listen to his account. In many parts of the Christian church the Eucharist was all conducted in Latin but in our part of the world we follow the Celtic tradition and so use the language of the people, which we call Anglo Saxon. The story that unfolded was the account of Jesus asleep in one of his follower's fishing boat, when a huge storm arose on the sea. The storm raged on for what seemed like hours and still, their master slept on through it. Did he not care about their situation? In the end the apostles decided to rouse Jesus and told him about their perilous plight. Gregory drew the story to its conclusion.

"Oh you of little faith," said Jesus. Then addressing the storm he said calmly, "Be still." Immediately the sea was still and no one would have known there had been a storm as it was so peaceful. The apostles were amazed and stared at each other wondering who this person was that even the wind and the waves obeyed his command."

After Gregory had finished, the Abbot gave a short speech about the meaning of this Gospel reading. He said it was a metaphor for our lives and that we would have times when things would not go well for us. When that happens we must not hesitate to call on Jesus in our prayers and He will be there to calm all our fears. He smiled and said he hoped that we would not need to call on Him to help us during our crossing to Inner Farne but, if we needed to, we shouldn't hesitate to ask Him. We looked at each other with our unspoken fears etched on our foreheads.

Our concerns were only transitory as we all skipped down to the jetty, eager to become young sailors. We were brought down to earth by father's stentorian voice booming across the still island air, as he implored us to be careful travellers and he dutifully laid out the safety procedures on board this craft. We were joined by Gregory, looking quite sinister in his jet black Benedictine habit, as he pulled his cowl over his head to protect him from the biting north wind, that he knew we would encounter when we left the security of the harbour and ventured into open waters.

However there was not a sinister bone in Gregory's body, as he was one of the most gentle people I have ever met in my short life. His voice is soft and soothing and his handsome face reflects the love he has for his creator. He is also a mine of information about the local geography of the Farne Islands. He told us that the Farnes were a group of islands off the coast of Northumberland. Apparently there are between fifteen and twenty islands depending on the state of the tides. Like the causeway that connects Lindisfarne to the mainland, sometimes some of the islands are submerged and then reveal themselves at low tide. The islands are scattered between one and five miles from the mainland. They are divided into two groups: Inner and Outer Farne. Outer Farnes include the islands of Staple, Brownsman, North and South Wamses, Big Hacar and the Longstone. Our destination was to be to the inner group of island which include the Megstone, Knoxes Reef and East and West Wideopens which are joined to each other at low tide. But we would land on Inner Farne itself where Aidan and Cuthbert made it their home when they wanted some peace and quiet from the hurly burly of monastic life.

We were enthralled at Gregory's knowledge and, shortly after his recount, we were ready to disembark onto the remote island. Father was first to alight from our boat as he leapt onto the embankment and skilfully secured the craft to a wooden stake. Obviously, from the high level of skill demonstrated, he had done this before and his strong arms held the side of the boat firmly, in order to enable everyone to safely alight.

We were not quite prepared for the welcome committee which awaited us. As our group assembled itself, we were deafened by a cacophony of squawking and squealing birds of every variety, size and coloured plumage. The more aggressive birds swooped and fluttered their wings at us in a show of bravado that the fiercest of warriors would be proud of. We raised our hands to protect ourselves but it was Gregory who once again showed us the depth of his knowledge.

"It's all right children, don't be afraid," he said reassuringly. "It's just a show of strength from the birds. Try not to react to them. It's difficult, I know, but they are just protecting their nests and young. Once they realise we are not a threat they will leave us alone." His words were calm and did reassure us and after a while proved also to be true.

Soon Gregory was able to demonstrate his grasp of ornithology as he drew our attention to the various species of birds. He pointed out three types of duck: Mallard, Shelduck and Eider. Terns were also in evidence including the Sandwich, Roseate and Arctic terns. I particularly like the Guillemots and Razorbills. Our arrival on the island created even more than avian interest as a small colony of grey seals swam in and beached themselves near our boat. Father warned us not to approach them, as their razor like teeth could quite easily sever one of our limbs. As we approached the centre of the island Gregory showed us some cuddly Puffins and told us that both the birds and rabbits use the same burrows, at different times, to nest.

We found the rough stone building which Aidan and Cuthbert had used, with only the birds and seals for company. Perhaps they would catch the odd rabbit to put in a pot, otherwise their diet consisted of what vegetation they could scratch together after exhausting what meagre supplies they brought from Lindisfarne. We used the building for our more substantial picnic, in order to protect ourselves from the scavenging birds. Gregory had overseen the preparation of cutlets of lamb which he had cut as thin as possible, together with some freshly baked bread. There were pats of fresh butter with which we could lavish the bread. Joseph had the idea of putting some meat between two pieces of bread, which he called a sandwich. I nodded my approval in recognition of an idea which was so obviously ahead of its time. The repast was washed down with a diluted form of mead which tasted sweet and cold and refreshed us for our afternoon of play and exploration of the island.

Gradually and quite unconsciously we all found ourselves seeking the solitude of the island and I sat on a narrow craggy outcrop in total wonderment at the beauty of it all. Quite spontaneously I found myself singing the praises of God in words I had not previously used,

New praise be given
to Christ newly crowned,
who back to his heaven

a new way has found;

God's blessedness sharing

before us he goes,

what mansions preparing,

what endless repose!

His glory still praising

on thrice holy ground,

the apostles stood gazing,

his mother around;

with hearts that beat faster,

with eyes full of love,

they watched while their master

ascended above.

I stood in total surrender to God, raising my hands heavenward toward the sun. From the haze that surrounded the orange orb walked a familiar figure. Although not known by name, it was the person or presence I had encountered at the well. Though I was not frightened he reassured me.

"Bede, don't be afraid. Remember what I told you about Pentecost. You will know when the time is right to tell your father. But before then you must be strong. Your father will need all your reserves of faith over the coming weeks. He will be tested but you must show him that God has not abandoned him. You are called to be a special friend of God and you will be given the right words to say. Only believe!"

At that moment my attention was diverted by a more familiar voice. It was Joseph and he sounded urgent.

"Bede, were you asleep?" he said, "Your dad and Gregory told me to find you as we are getting ready to go back to Lindisfarne. I didn't think that you had nodded off." He looked perplexed that anyone could possibly sleep in such an inhospitable place.

I rubbed my eyes, more in disbelief at my vision rather than sleep but I knew it would be pointless to deny the evidence of Joseph's own eyes. All the way back to our home destination I had to withstand taunts from the rest of the party. I smiled back at them in an effort to disguise my confusion and consternation about the revelations of my mysterious messenger.

Back on Lindisfarne our day was not quite over. Gregory had to hurry off to church for the service of Vespers but he told us all to be back at the bay in an hour as he had a surprise for us. We duly obliged and, although our stomachs were rumbling, as it was now some hours since we had devoured our picnic on Inner Farne, we all gathered in the bay overlooking the North Sea in the fading light.

We were greeted by our host Gregory who was grilling fish he had caught, on a fire of driftwood. He handed our meals to us on wooden plates garnished by long thin strips of a fried vegetable. He informed us that they were parsnips which were absolutely delicious. We all ate voraciously.

"This is what I call my signature dish, my speciality." he proclaimed proudly, "Fish and chips!"

Gertrude oohed her appreciation and thanked Gregory for his surprise.

"Don't mention it Gertrude but that is not my surprise. I want you to look there, out to sea," said Gregory pointing out to the horizon with his bony right index finger.

I craned my neck so that I could see past Joseph's blonde hair and there I saw the most beautiful sky I have ever witnessed. Greens and blues vied with oranges, yellows and reds to provide a stunning array of colours. The light played a silent tune with an octave of vivid colours. Adults and children alike, gasped in wonderment as Gregory enhanced his already tall stature by standing on a rock and waving towards the display exclaiming,

"May I present, the Aurora Borealis, also known as the Northern Lights!" Before we could form a question and realising our ignorance he launched into his explanation.

He told us that the Aurora is an incredible light show caused by the collisions between electrically charged particles released from the sun, that enter the earth's atmosphere and collide with gases such as oxygen and nitrogen. The lights are seen around the magnetic poles of the northern and southern hemispheres. Although most of us believe that the world is flat, Gregory says he thinks the world is a sphere. We live in the northern half and he believes this light show may be mirrored in the southern hemisphere too.

"I have watched these lights for many winters and springs and my study of the stars and science have led me to these conclusions. I know the Church is not comfortable about the study of the sciences but I can only say that science confirms to me the glory of God and His magnificent creation. Who can deny the wonder of our God when you look at those lights?"

No one could disagree with Gregory and replete from our supper and buoyed by my mysterious encounter on Inner Farne and with the glorious sight of the Aurora Borealis, I praised God on my bed that night as I reflected on the wonder of my being. I also thought about the information imparted to me by the mysterious stranger on Inner Farne. His warning that my father was about to have his faith tested and that I would have to be a beacon of light for him. It was not by accident that Gregory had chosen to present us with a representation of God's own light in the form of the Aurora Borealis. A light that darkness can not overpower!

Chapter Ten

Captured

The days following our visit to Inner Farne were filled with a mixture of morning work (mainly fetching and carrying for my father) and afternoon play consisting of kickbladder, fishing and general exploration of the island. Our day was punctuated by the sound of the monastery bell, summoning us to meals prefaced by some sort of religious service. We didn't seem to mind this prelude to our repasts and indeed it only served to increase our anticipation of the delicious food that was to follow.

The monks' day would begin earlier than ours as they would rise at around 5 am when they would prepare for their first service of Vigils in the church at 6 am. They would usually read from the Book of Psalms. A second service called Lauds or morning prayer would happen at around 7.15 am. We would sometimes get up for this service, as breakfast would take place after Lauds. The monks would sing their morning prayers. The bell would summon us at noon for Midday Prayer before lunch at 12.30 pm. After lunch, the monks were given free time which was when Gregory would play kickbladder with us or show us the best fishing places on the island. The bell would again ring at 5 pm for more prayers called Vespers, followed by the main meal of the day, supper, at 6.30 pm. A period of quiet reflection time after supper culminated in the final night prayer service of Compline at 8.15 pm. The monks are then not supposed to speak until Lauds the next day. However this was too much for us to observe as we used to whisper the night away in our bunks until we dropped off to sleep.

The regimented nature of our days was a comfort to us and gave some structure to our lives. Our time on the island was drawing to a close but on the penultimate day of our stay something was about to happen that would impact upon all our lives.

We had just finished lunch of roast fish, followed by a pudding of apple pie washed down by diluted mead. Joseph, Odin and I scampered across the sand dunes with our kickbladder. Gregory could not join us as he was behind in his work of copying the Lindisfarne Gospel and so was making use of the excellent light, which would facilitate his scribing. Gertrude stayed behind to play with a young girl who had come over from the mainland with her mother, bearing provisions for the monks. We were playing on the north west side of the island, where the sands were almost perfectly flat and sheltered from the blast from the prevailing easterly winds, whipping in from the North Sea. Joseph suggested a game of three pots in and volunteered to go in goal. He was on top form, diving to his left and right keeping out all our shots. The idea was that the first to score three goals would take his turn in goal.

Joseph was just retrieving the kickbladder, after having tipped Odin's shot round the post, when our game was interrupted by an ear piecing persistent metallic clanging. At first we looked at each other in disbelieve until the clanging became even more urgent. We realised this was the dinner bell which usually summoned us to lunch or dinner but had suddenly transformed itself into a discordant alarm bell. Instinctively we all responded, leaving the kickbladder lying forlornly half way up a sand dune and ran towards the noise. We negotiated the steep bank of a small hillock and then descended from the peak, accelerating down to where a knot of people had gathered. We could see Gregory pounding the bell as if he were trying to wake the dead.

"Thank you Gregory, I think we are all here," said the Abbot scanning the multitude and mentally ticking off the names in an imaginary register. "Now take the Gospel, the original, and hide it where we have discussed."

Gregory did not require a second invitation and he quit tolling the bell and ran and disappeared into the monastery building. The other monks were anxiously whispering to one another, there faces grim with worry. We were confused at this kerfuffle and and I looked at my father imploring him to explain. In response he slowly lifted his left arm and pointed out to sea. Only then did I realise that all of the assembled throng too were following my father's direction and looking in an easterly direction, out into the white spume of the North Sea. I could see four figures about to beach a long boat on to the shore. My father spoke very deliberately and only one word.

"Vikings!"

This word was sufficient to send shudders through the bones of most Northumbrians. Stories surrounding the raiders from over the North Sea were legion, though how many of them were actually true no one was sure. My father was always very philosophical about them and indeed Odin's parents were descended from them. My father always said that the letters of fear spelt out - false expectations appearing real and that we should not fear what we do not know. However most Northumbrians feared that, these isolated raids would be replaced by a full scale invasion. For the first time I saw the signs of anxiety etched on my father's face, as he carefully watched their progress across the sand and towards our congregation.

Soon there stood before us four huge men clad in animal skins and bearing swords. One of them, who assumed the leadership, stepped forward and exclaimed,

"*Mad, vi ønsker, Mad, vi ønsker.*" He brandished his weapon threateningly and watched as we looked confused one to another. "*Mad, vi ønsker Mad, vi ønsker*" He grimaced at the Abbot and then stood head to head with my father and repeated, "*Mad, vi ønsker. mad eller du alle dø*" His manner became increasingly threatening, especially towards my father and I began to fear for his safety. Just then a younger voice, and in the same language, broke the deadlock.

"*Jeg kan få dig mad, men undlad venligst at dræbe os,*" said Odin pushing himself between the Viking and my father. "*Giv mig dit ord At vi vil være sikker, og jeg vil få dig mad."* The leader looked surprised at this upstart then roared with laughter.

"Ja ja lidt Viking Vi ønsker ikke at dræbe nogen. Vi er bare sulten." exclaimed the leader who then shared the joke with his compatriots who joined him in a hearty laugh. Odin thought now would be an opportune time to translate for his friends. Looking round the group he explained,

"It's okay, they mean us no harm they just want food. I suggest we get together some supplies, enough to fill the boat, and take them down to the shore. Hopefully this will get rid of them." This suggestion was taken up and a crocodile of people soon depleted the monks' larder and transported the contents down to the boat, which was almost filled. Our unwelcome guest carefully adjusted the load on the boat, so the risk of capsizing was diminished. He even discarded a number of boxes and threw them onto the shore. His three compatriots sat themselves down so that they could access their oars whilst their leader stood eyeing us. Looking at Odin he beckoned him to come on board.

"Hvordan, hvor lidt Viking er det tid til at komme hjem." commanded the blonde Viking.

"nej, nej, jeg bor her" protested Odin.

"Ja lidt Viking du skal kunne lide. Dit navn er Odin. Du er en gud min søn. Behøver jeg at true dine venner? Som nu, eller skal jeg nødt til at dræbe

dem." The Viking's tone and manner were not to be disobeyed. Odin turned away from him and once again translated.

"I must go with them or they will kill all of you. Please tell mam and dad I love them." Father stepped forward to try to prevent him from going but Odin's mind was set and father could only watch as he boarded the craft, tears streaming down both their cheeks. We watched helplessly as the long boat slid effortlessly into the offing and out into open water and approached the horizon, like a Viking sea burial ship.

I looked at my father in his utter desolation and I felt that I some how had to become the parent and minister to my own father. It was he who had been the instigator of the journey to Lindisfarne, he who had reassured Joseph's and Odin's parents that all would be well. Now that burden bore down heavily upon him, like Christ's cross on the way to Calvary. The Abbot and Gregory came across and consoled father who could only shake his head in despair and disbelief. After they all had moved off back to the monastery, where life would again resume its unerring pattern, I approached father and put my arm round his shoulders.

"Dad!" I said reassuringly, "remember the story of Joseph in the Bible and how it tells us that God was with him in all his trials and tribulations." I thought that I detected a glimmer of response in his dulled eyes as he struggled to recall the details of the story.

*   *   *   *   *   *

Joseph's father, Jacob, had twelve sons but Joseph was his favourite. He was born to his true wife Rebecca late on in their marriage after they both thought that she was unable to have children. She went on to have a second son Benjamin but as Joseph was the first child of Rebecca he was held in high regard. His ten older brothers born to other women were not so keen on him, as they were jealous of the attention he got and, it has to be said, Joseph's attitude towards them did not help.

One day when he was seventeen he went out to join his elder brothers who were tending the sheep. His brothers wore short coats with no sleeves, so that their arms and legs were free for hard work. Jacob had a special coat made for Joseph; a coat of many colours. It was a long coat with sleeves and showed that Joseph was a master and not just a common worker like his brothers. This made them even more jealous of Joseph and they began to hate him.

This was made even worse when Joseph told them about his dreams:

"I dreamed that we were binding sheaves of corn at harvest time. My sheaf stood up tall and straight. All your sheaves bowed down to mine. I also dreamed that the sun and moon and eleven stars bowed down before me."

'What!" cried his brothers,"Does this mean that you're going to lord it over us?" And they hated Joseph even more and plotted to get rid of him. Even Jacob his father was taken aback by Joseph's dreams but he knew he would be a wise man one day. In the meantime he sent him out one day to help his brothers in the field. They saw his coat of many colours a long way off,

"Here comes the dreamer, let's kill him and throw his body into a pit. We'll tell father that a wild animal seized him." But God was with Joseph and Reuben, the the eldest brother, intervened and said not to kill him but just put him into the pit. He hoped to rescue Joseph later when his brothers had cooled down.

When Joseph came they tore off his coat and put him in a deep pit dug into the ground. Then they sat down to eat whilst Reuben left to do another job. Not long after some merchants came by with spices to sell in Egypt.

"Let's sell Joseph to these merchants," said one brother, "Then we need not kill him, after all he is our brother." They all agreed and sold Joseph to the merchants and when Reuben returned he was shocked at the brothers' actions. Nevertheless he had to go along with the brothers' story when they took the coat of many colours, dipped in goat's blood, back to their father.

"Look father! Isn't this the coat you gave to Joseph. A wild beast must have seized him!"

No one could comfort Jacob in his grief, for he believed that Joseph was dead. But Joseph was alive - a slave in Egypt.

But God was with Joseph. The merchants sold Joseph as a slave in Egypt. He was bought by Potiphar, a captain in the Royal Guard. He soon found that Joseph was a wise man. He put him in charge of his whole household. But his wife told lies about Joseph and so Potiphar sent him to the royal prison.

But God was with Joseph, even in prison. The keeper of the prison found how wise Joseph was too. He put Joseph in charge of the prisoners. Among them were the butler and the baker of Pharaoh the king. One morning they both looked sad,

"Each of us has had a dream," they told Joseph, "But we do not know what they mean."

"My God has made me wise," replied Joseph, "I can tell you the meaning of your dreams. But I ask you if my interpretations are true, then tell Pharaoh and he may well release me too" They both agreed and the butler was first to tell Joseph his dream.

"In my dream," said the butler,"I saw a vine with three bunches of grapes. I pressed them into Pharaoh's cup and gave the cup of wine into his hand."

"The three bunches are three days," said Joseph, "In three days Pharaoh will forgive you and you will be serving him wine again. Now master baker tell me your dream." Boosted by what Joseph had told the butler, the baker began,

"I was carrying three baskets of white bread on my head and the birds were eating out of the top of the basket," said the baker. However the news for the prisoner was not good.

"I am afraid the dream means that in three days Pharaoh will have you hanged!"

Three days later Pharaoh had his baker put to death. He forgave the butler. However the butler forgot all about Joseph and the agreement he had made. Joseph lay in prison for two more years but God was with him all the time and Joseph was soon to have a change of circumstances.

One night Pharaoh, King of Egypt, dreamt that he stood by the river and seven fat cows came out of the water and chewed grass in the meadow. Then seven thin cows came out of water. They ate up the seven fat cows, but they were just as thin as before! Whatever did it mean? Pharaoh was very worried. None of his wise men could explain his dream. Then the butler remembered Joseph and so he was sent for and Pharaoh asked him,

"I hear that you are wise and can explain dreams?"

"It is not me," said Joseph. "My God speaks through me." So Pharaoh told him the dream and Joseph explained it."God has shown you what is to come Pharaoh. There will be seven fat years with plenty of food. Then there will be seven thin years of hunger when people will forget the fat years of plenty. Therefore let Pharaoh set a wise man to rule over Egypt.

He can store food in the years of plenty and so have food for the years of hunger."

Pharaoh was amazed and said, "Truly God has filled you with wisdom. I will set you over all Egypt. Here is my ring to show that you rule for me." Then Joseph rode throughout Egypt in the royal chariot and the people bowed down before Joseph the ruler of all Egypt.

For seven years there was plenty of food. Joseph stored up corn all over the land of Egypt. Then came seven years without rain. There was hunger in many lands, except Egypt, and people went down to Egypt to buy corn. Among them were the elder brothers of Joseph.

Joseph knew his brothers at once but they did not recognise him. Joseph accused them of being spies so that he could keep one of them in prison, in order that they would bring their younger brother Benjamin to see him. It was just a trick because Joseph was planning to reunite the whole family again in Egypt.

On the next trip they brought Benjamin but, before they went home, Joseph hid his silver cup in Benjamin's sack. When he was caught Benjamin was ordered to stay in Egypt as a slave but the brothers protested that this would break the heart of their father Jacob. Then Joseph could hide his secret no longer and with tears of joy he told his brothers who he was. He bade them hurry home and bring back Jacob with them.

So Jacob and his whole family came to Egypt and Joseph welcomed them with tears of happiness. The whole family were reunited once again and lived in safety and prosperity with Joseph in Egypt.

God had truly been with Joseph all this time.

*   *   *   *   *   *

Although my father knew this story well, the finer details were lost on him as he struggled to come to terms with the loss of Odin. I had to reinforce the point of the story and do it quickly before this test of his faith became a crisis of faith.

"Dad through it all, his slavery, his wrongful arrest, his imprisonment and his time in a foreign land, the Bible tells us that God was always with Joseph and he prospered in everything he did. So it will be with Odin; God will be with him. You must believe this! We must believe this!"

I firmly held on to his arm and pressed it in reassurance and father slowly nodded his assent, tears silently streaming from his eyes. For the first time in my life I saw doubt etched in my father's face and the words of the mysterious being I had met on Inner Farne came to mind. I knew that I had to be strong, that I had to be a boy, or man, of faith. The wind snaked the sand across the beach like a sidewinder, as we gazed out to the horizon and I quietly prayed under my breath,

"Odin, God is with you...God is with you."

Chapter Eleven

The Return

Our final day saw father concluding his work in the monastery in utter silence and with him forgoing meals, which again were taken in a similar silence. I had never seen him chop wood and hammer nails in with such force and he completed his duties by mid afternoon and we began packing for our return journey home, early the next day. Our play too was curtailed, as none of us had any more appetite for games and the attractions of the island had lost their allure. The kickbladder lay lonely in the wisps of long bent grass growing out of the sand dunes, an uncomfortable reminder of what had transpired the previous day. Gregory tried to keep our spirits up but a long day eventually drew to a close with the Aurora Borealis giving way to a beautiful red sky, illuminating the infinite panorama of the North Sea. I slept fitfully, with the sound of an imaginary alarm bell interrupting my disturbing dreams. After what seemed like hours of lonely blackness, I eventually fell into a deep sleep.

The red sky of the previous night did indeed bode well for our new day. Northumbrian shepherds would surely be delighted by the clear, crisp cloudless morning, as the waters surrounding this holiest of islands receded and revealed the safe track to the mainland. Our cart was packed, though not as fully laden as it would have been - our Viking "friends" had seen to that. Father was embarrassed to take so much of the monastery's provisions and protested to the Abbot. However the cleric insisted that he be rewarded for his work, explaining that they could soon replenish stocks with the Lord's, and their mainland friends', help. Reluctantly father agreed and with head hung low he began his farewells to the monks he knew so well. As he stumbled and mumbled his adieus the Abbot, seeing his difficulty in finding the right words, came to his aid.

"Edwin...Edwin my son," he said grasping his shoulders. "You must not blame yourself for the loss of Odin. It was not your fault. It could have happened to him at Jarrow or anywhere. There has been the odd Viking raid up and down the coast. Even as far down as our monastery at Whitby."

"Father Abbot....what am I to say....to say to his parents?" replied father with the agony of anticipation etched across his face. "It was I who brought him here, it was I who was responsible for him. Tell me Father what am I to say?"

Father Abbot nodded sagely and looked father straight in the eye,

"Listen Edwin. What distinguishes us from those Vikings is that we believe in the one true living God. We believe that He has us in the palm of His hands. He has our well being in mind at all times. Into His hands you must put the boy Odin. He will care for Him. Edwin, your faith has seen you through to this point and your faith will see you through this crisis too. You are a good man Edwin. The Lord will give you the words to say to the boy's parents. You must stay strong in faith for their sakes and for the sake of your own family. Now may God go with you and until we meet again."

He embraced my father and allowed the cowl of his habit to soak up his silent tears. Father picked up Gertrude and swung her onto the cart as we waved our muted goodbyes to the monks and trundled across the causeway to the mainland. We took one last look at the hazy outline of the island as we turned down the tree lined track to Bamburgh.

Unlike the journey to the island it was not necessary to break the journey at Bamburgh and so we pressed on to Alnmouth where we would have our first over night stop on the return leg. The journey passed uneventfully and largely in silence as the cart creaked its way along the coastal path. We watched the outline of Bamburgh Castle disappear into the background. We broke for a lunch of bread and cheese a couple of miles outside of the town. Father obviously did not wish to encounter any of the locals, who he knew would now be familiar with the events of forty eight hours ago. We munched on the food provided for us by the monks and soon gathered the scraps (which did not fill quite as many baskets as in the feeding of the five thousand) and prepared to complete the first leg of our journey before nightfall. The gloom of the gathering dusk reflected our feelings as we saw the outline of uncle's house. Smoke filtered its way into the greying sky and we all anticipated the meal that Aunt Agnes may have prepared for us. We felt guilty that we should think of our stomachs at a time like this, nevertheless our anticipation was gaining confirmation, as we neared the habitation, from the smells that were filling the evening air.

Aelred greeted father with a knowing nod then embraced him without uttering a single word. Aunt Agnes joined them in a three way hug, tears flowing down her cheeks. The bush telegraph had obviously outpaced us and truly bad news does travel quickly and no words of explanation were requested nor needed. Agnes, now fully showing the outline of her child, pulled away from the small throng and greeted the children standing there in confusion.

"Now children, you must be so tired. And hungry I'll be bound?" she said holding back the tears and beckoning us all inside their welcoming abode. Soon we were all washed and fed and bedded down. We could hear the hushed voices of father and my aunt and uncle and, from time to time, the obvious sounds of father breaking down as he related the story to them, no doubt piling the guilt of what had happened upon himself. Eventually sleep took over and we soon found ourselves oblivious to father's self recriminations and his in-laws invocations not to blame himself.

Next day we packed our things quickly, said our farewells and embarked on the second leg of our journey. Aunt Agnes reminded father that she would visit us on Tyneside in order to give birth with the help of her sister, my mother. She asked too if he would still be godfather to her new offspring. This seemed to cheer father up and with one final embrace we set off. I glanced up at the cross on top of the hill overlooking the bay and sent a prayer up to heaven for our safe return. The rest of our journey over the next two days was just one mighty trudge, as we wound our way down the Northumberland coast and to the ferry over the Tyne. Any encounter with passing strangers were met with a perfunctory nod and grunt from my father. Meals were taken only as a necessary means of refuelling us for the remainder of the journey and taken largely in silence. Soon we found ourselves on the Tyne and quickly disembarked on the southern bank. The animal and cart trundled its way back to our homestead where father left us to hurriedly explain events to mother in the privacy of the inside of our home. We waited patiently until they both emerged, clearly distressed. Father said,

"Bede, I would like you to see to the ass and cart and Gertrude, I want you to help him get the things inside. Joseph, I will take you home. Then I must see Odin's parents."

I nodded my agreement and before I could have made any progress he and Joseph had disappeared down the track. We completed our tasks and two hours later father returned, even more distressed, to be comforted by mother. Gertrude and I gave our parents the time and space they needed at this difficult time. I remembered the words spoken to me by the mysterious being on Inner Farne and indeed I would be required to be strong and draw on my reserves of faith. Father had taught me well, now it was my turn to repay him.

Chapter Twelve

School

It is now a month since Odin was kidnapped from us and Lent has concluded with Good Friday and we celebrated the great feast of the Lord's resurrection just two days ago on Easter Sunday. I always associate the days following Easter with bright, sun shiny, spring weather. Although the weather is indeed dry and bright and the vivid yellow daffodils are scattered randomly across the Tyne valley, there is still a shadow casting its length over our family.

Things have assumed a degree of normality but my father is still not his usual self. He is quiet and withdrawn and, although she does not say so, I know that my mother is worried about him. Her nagging level towards him has definitely reduced but we children often bare the brunt of her temper and so we ensure that our chores are always up to date. Father's friendship with Tor however seems to have deepened and they can often be seen in deep conversation. This contrasts with his wife Freyja's attitude towards my father. She is brusque and sharp with him, her eyes avoiding contact at all times.

Today we resumed our studies with Godric in a small anteroom at St. Paul's Monastery Jarrow. As I have said, Godric began teaching a few of us to read and write about a year ago. He had agreed to the continuation of this tuition for the three boys Bede, Joseph and Odin. However, as we were now one short he has agreed with father to include Gertrude in our lessons, much to my mother's chagrin.

"What do girls want with all that learning nonsense?" she protested to father. "How will that help her to keep house and put food on the table for you men folk? I have never learned to read or write and I can still make a rabbit pie. It's never done me any harm. I don't know. What with all your fancy ideas. Girls reading and writing indeed!"

"Hilda, Hilda!" my father shook his head in despair, "It does not matter if our children are boys or girls, it is good for them to have an education. We want them to do better than us in life. Mark my words times are changing and one thing those Romans left us is the importance of a good education."

On this my father was not to be deterred and so here we are, a threesome waiting to be educated by our eager young monk. Godric is a red haired man of around twenty five summers or so, with a pleasing face and a happy demeanour.

'Good morning children." He greets us with the friendly air of an uncle not too remote in age from us. An uncle who knows how the world works and who is able to impart his enthusiasm for learning. "I think we will begin with some basic Latin verbs in order to blow away the cobwebs from your brains, as it is a number of weeks since we last met."

We were quite familiar with the basic Latin verbs having begun our studies several months earlier and it was with anticipation that we awaited Godric's favourite joke, which would initiate my sister Gertrude to our proceedings.

"Right Bede! Would you like to conjugate the verb to love – amo?" asked Godric. I could feel Gertrude's anxious eyes darting from Godric then to me, to Joseph then back to me and thus with ramrod back I stood up and began my conjugation.

"Amo, amas, amat, amamus, amatis, amant," I recited looking pleased with myself. I nodded to Godric and without invitation I sat down and awaited my friend taking up the gauntlet.

"Now you Joseph," requested Godric and Joseph proceeded to repeat my conjugation and we waited with baited breath as he turned to my sister,

"ditto Gertrude."

"Ditto, dittas, dittat, dittamus, dittatis, dittant," she uttered confidently, a smirk of self satisfaction growing across her face. We all collapsed in hilarity at her naive entrapment by Godric. A trap we all had fallen into in the past. But Gertrude, not realising her mistake, took the only action she knew. She burst into tears! This took the monk aback and with a look of panic on his face, at his joke having backfired, he began to try to make amends for his insensitivity.

Godric then proceeded to spend most of the next hour in pacifying Gertrude and explaining to her that ditto was not a Latin verb but just meant the same. So he was asking her to conjugate the same verb, amo, as Joseph and I had conjugated. He went on to explain that, this was his little joke that he played on all his students and that she was not to take this too seriously. We sat impassively with a guilty look of the conspirator upon our faces. In retrospect I feel there was more we could have done in backing up Godric's story by confessing that we had fallen victim too but we both kept quiet. I couldn't help wondering what would happen to me when I got home if he failed to win my sister round. Eventually he calmed her down and we resumed our Latin studies for the remaining time we had. Gertrude actually showed quite an aptitude for the language and by the end of the lesson she was not too far behind us in her knowledge.

It has to be said that Godric is not always so understanding and everyone knows about his vocabulary tests which he calls his 'seventeen out of twenty tests.' This is the pass mark and if you do not achieve this then you are destined to repeat the test until you do so. Gertrude passed with flying colours whilst Joseph and I had to repeat the test a second time. This helped to redress the balance. She sat with her hands tucked under her chin, patiently waiting for us to complete the test and then looked on rather smugly as we awaited Godric's re-marking. Gradually the marks crept up and I improved from sixteen to nineteen whereas Joseph managed to get full marks. We were ecstatic that we had accomplished the passmark, albeit at the second attempt but Gertrude indeed had had the last laugh on us.

After several hours of hard work it was time to clear our things away and time also to discuss our feelings about our missing friend. It was Godric who broached the subject with us.

"You must all be missing your friend Odin so much. Your father especially must be feeling dreadful. How is he? I haven't had the opportunity to speak with him yet. And how are Odin's parents -Tor and Freyja isn't it? How are they coping?" He sat down on a bench near the window as if to invite us all to confide in him.

We too made ourselves comfortable on the opposite bench and I explained how I felt that father was bearing the guilt of what had occurred himself, although everyone had said how it could have happened to any of us at any time. I told him how he and Tor seemed to be friends still but how Odin's mother Freya was cold and distant. How we were all walking on egg shells with mother and how my aunt and uncle would, hopefully, soon be coming down from Alnmouth for the birth of their child. And how I felt that this may have a helpful effect on our family.

Godric sagely nodded his head in understanding and I could tell that he was thinking of some suitable words to comfort us.

"You know Odin is very precious, as are you all, to God," said Godric and to reinforce his point he pulled a leather bound book from the shelf and read us this story from the Gospel of St. Luke in the New Testament:

"An argument started amongst the disciples as to which of them would be the greatest. Jesus knowing their thoughts, took a little child and made her stand beside him. Then he said to them,

"Whoever welcomes this little child in my name welcomes me; and whoever welcomes me welcomes the one who sent me. For she or he who is the least among you all - she or he is the greatest." Then Jesus continued, "I tell you the truth, unless you change and become like little children, you will never enter the kingdom of heaven....And whoever welcomes a little child like this in my name welcomes me. But if anyone causes one of these little ones to sin, it would be better for him to have a large millstone hung around his neck and be drowned in the depths of the sea. See that you do not look down on one of these little ones. For I tell you that their angels in heaven always see the face of my father in heaven."

Godric looked up from the book and then said reassuringly, "See children, God has provided a guardian angel to look after Odin whilst he is away from us. Jesus tells that God really cares for children." Then looking back down at the book he concluded the story.

'What do you think? If a man owns a hundred sheep and one of them wanders away, will he not leave the ninety nine on the hills and go and look for the one that wandered off? And if he finds it, I tell you the truth, he is happier about that one sheep than about the ninety nine that did not wander off. In the same way your Father in heaven is not willing that any of these little ones should be lost."

Godric slammed the book shut and a cloud of dust billowed up into the air. We all sat upright in fright as he said, "So, God has not forgotten about Odin. He is with him, but we must still pray for him always and I am sure all will work out for the best. Put him in God's hand." We all agreed that we would continue in prayer for him. Godric carefully placed the book back on the shelf and then clasped his hands and changing the subject said,

"What about the kickbladder tournament? How are things going? What about the girls? You know that I am part of the committee organising the tournament. As well as four teams from our area there are more teams coming from afar." He seemed pleased with the progress he was making and continued,"There is one team coming from near our monastery in Monkwearmouth and another from across the River Wear; the Sunter Land it's called. So the competition will be fierce, therefore you need to make sure you are well prepared."

We explained how Agatha had taken over the management of our team and how she had introduced us to the girls Jane, Helen, Mary and Teresa. We told him how good they were but that the silky skills of Odin were still a very big miss. We'd had a couple of training sessions and we were meeting again tomorrow. I could see that Godric was impressed and with that he dismissed us and we all returned home feeling happier that God had Odin, and our future in His hands.

Chapter Thirteen
Girls, Girls, Girls

It is Saturday before the feast of Ascension and we have all assembled for a kickbladder training session under the watchful eye of our manager Agatha. She really put us through our paces, not only concentrating on our skills but also on our fitness. She devised what she called a circuit of activities, which involved a lot of bending, stretching and running. It was a full hour of these activities and we had not even kicked a bladder. At last Agatha whistled to us all that she wanted us to gather round her, for a team talk. We were a full complement of those players available: me, Joseph, Caedmon, Eldrick, their cousins Alfred and Christopher and their friends Tobias and James plus the four girls Jane, Helen, Mary and Teresa. One notable absentee of course was our playmaker and goalscorer Odin.

Agatha stood with her hands on hips in control of our situation and when she had commanded total silence, solely by her stare, she began her explanation. There would be sixteen teams taking part in the tournament coming from villages around Tyneside and Wearside. There would be four groups of three teams. Each team would get two points for a win and one point for a draw and the top two teams would go forward to the last eight teams which, through two further knock out rounds, would leave two teams in the final. That would mean that, if we managed to get to the final, we would have to play a total of six games. Each game would be split into two halves with each half lasting for as long as the sand ran out of the timer; this would probably take about ten minutes.

"So I am sure you will agree that we will have to be fully fit, if we are to get through to the final and win the tournament," she said. "There will be seven players in each team and there must be at least two girls on the field at all times. We have ten players so we will change the players around between games and even during the games. Odin will be a big miss but we just have to get on with it, we should try and win it for his sake." We all murmured our agreement as she continued, "The tournament will take place the day after Pentecost Sunday, as part of celebration of the great feast."

Caedmon was anxiously waiting for her to finish and when he found an opportune time he interjected, "Have you though about who should be the leader of the team...our captain?" Ever since my little chat with him he had taken his duties as our leader most seriously but now he sensed that Agatha may not have the same opinion of him as me.

"Don't worry Caedmon I have seen how well you support the other players and I need someone on the pitch who can put into play the plans I have. I think you are that person." she smiled reassuringly and he noticeably relaxed into the grassy bank behind him. "However I think that Helen has a practical suggestion which I feel may give us an edge over the other teams." She turned towards the young girl and, with a slight motion of her eyebrows, invited her to address the assembled team. She was a dark haired girl who had impressed the boys with her skills as a defensive player. She confidently stood next to Agatha and said,

"I thought that it would be a good idea if we all wore the same outfit. It would make us look more like a team and more organised and would give the impression to the other teams that we meant business. It would also help us to identify our team mates more easily and make it easier to pass to one another." Helen enhanced what she said through various waving of her arms which had the effect of making her listeners think that she knew what she was talking about. We all looked from one to another and our nods of agreement became unanimous. Seeing that she had the team eating out of her hand she continued with the meat of her suggestion,"My aunt has some material we can have but the only thing is that we will have to make the outfits ourselves."

Eldrick was the first to comment,

"Just as well we have got some girls in our team! I knew they would come in handy!" We all guffawed with delight at his droll comment. Well I say all but, after our cheers had subsided, we saw the stony faces of the four girls, flanked by Agatha herself who replied,

"We are a team. We train together, we play together, we win together, we lose together and ....we sew together!" It was the girls' turn now to jeer and Agatha waved her hands to get control once again, "Many hands make light work and it will be good for you boys to learn some new skills."

In the days that followed, training consisted of three elements: fitness work, followed by game strategies (which Agatha called tactics) then sewing. I got to quite like the sewing element more than I ever thought I would. Helen's aunt supplied us with long lengths of white linen, with off cuts of red material. Each one in turn was measured for a length of the white linen and then strips of the red material were carefully sown on. The finished article was a tunic of red and white stripes, bound by a belt of hessian. We boys sat diligently, if slowly, working hard to finish off the tunics.

Helen's idea was taken up by the other teams who heard about it through manager meetings attended by Agatha. So the tournament will be a riot of colour.

Well done Helen! Great idea!

Chapter Fourteen

Ascension

The Easter season is very special to us Christians. After Jesus rose from the dead on Easter Sunday he began to appear to his followers, known as apostles, from time to time. Imagine how they must have felt. They had just seen the man they believed in, crucified on Good Friday. Jesus had told his apostles that it was necessary for him to suffer and to die but he told them that after three days he would rise from the dead.

I suppose in the horror and confusion of the death of Jesus it would be easy to understand that the apostles would forget or disbelieve what they had been told by their master. One of his apostles, Peter who had been his right hand man, even denied that he knew Jesus - three times! On that Easter day, and for weeks after, Jesus gradually revealed himself to those who he wanted to. There were two men who were walking to a nearby town called Emmaus and they were discussing what had happened over the past few days, no doubt filled with disbelief and fear. Jesus sidled up to them but they did not recognise Him. He asked them what was up and they were amazed that He did not know what had been happening. But it was Jesus who explained to them the meaning of the events and it eventually dawned on them, when He broke bread at a meal he shared with them, who this stranger really was.

Then there was the story of one of the apostles called Thomas. Jesus had appeared to the apostles but Thomas was not there. When he came back the rest excitedly told him what had happened. They were full of stories about how He had suddenly appeared to them in a locked room. Thomas shook his head at these fanciful stories and said,

"Unless I see for myself and actually put my fingers into the holes in Jesus' hands I will not believe."

Later on in the week the apostles were all together again in a locked room hiding from the Jewish people, who thought that they were dangerous followers of Jesus. They were praying and this time Thomas was with them. Just then there was the sound of a rushing wind and there in front of them stood Jesus. Thomas gasped in amazement and fell to his knees when Jesus extended his arms showing him the wounds from His death on the cross and inviting Thomas to put his fingers into them. In shame Thomas could only cry, "My Lord and my God." Thomas went on to be one of the greatest messengers telling people about Jesus, travelling all over the world. However to this day he is known as doubting Thomas.

Today, I am standing in the church of St. Paul's Jarrow where we are celebrating another great feast day for us Christians - The Ascension of the Lord. After Jesus had appeared to His friends he told them that He would have to go back to his Father in heaven. His followers didn't quite understand. We are about to hear Godric read an account of these events. He now moves to the lectern on the sanctuary of the church where he reads from the book of the Acts of the Apostles and tells what happened about 600 years ago. He begins:

"A reading from the Acts of the Apostles,
The eleven disciples went to Galilee, to the mountain where Jesus told them to go. When they saw him, they worshipped him; but some doubted. Then Jesus came to them and said,

"All authority in heaven and earth has been given to me. Therefore go and make disciples of all nations, baptising them in the name of the Father and of the Son and of the Holy Spirit and teaching them to obey everything I have commanded you. And surely I am with you always, to the very end of the age. Go back to the upper room and pray and fast. You will receive power when the Holy Spirit comes on you; and you will be my witnesses in Jerusalem, Judea and to the ends of the earth."

After he said this, he was taken up before their eyes, and a cloud hid him from their sight. They were looking intently up into the sky as he was going when suddenly two men dressed in white stood beside them and said,

"Men of Galilee, why do you stand here looking into the sky? This same Jesus, who has been taken from you into heaven, will come back in the same way you have seen him go into heaven."

Then they all return to Jerusalem from the hill called the Mount of Olives. When they arrived they went upstairs to the room where they were staying. They all joined together constantly in prayer, along with the women and Mary the mother of Jesus and with his brothers."

Godric breathed a sigh of relief at having accomplished the reading without any mistakes and looking up at the congregation concluded with the proclamation, "The Word of the Lord" and then climbed down from the dais.

We all replied in unison "Thanks be to God." and we sat down and awaited the sermon which was to be given by the acting Abbot of St. Paul's, Father Gerard.

"Brothers and sisters in Christ," he began. "We come together on this Thursday to celebrate this great feast. We have just heard how Jesus told the apostles to go away and fast and pray for the coming of the Holy Spirit We too should listen to these words and do the same for the next nine days, in order to welcome the Holy Spirit into our hearts at Pentecost."

That word Pentecost struck home to me like a spear through my soul. Pentecost was a great feast of harvest for the Jewish people thousands of years ago. It was when Jesus fulfilled his promise to the apostles and sent his Holy Spirit into their hearts in order to embolden them. It was also the word the mysterious stranger had used at the well. It was now time to tell father about what had been revealed to me at that special place. Following the service, the walk home along the banks of the Tyne would be the opportunity I needed.

After exchanging pleasantries with our friends and neighbours (Tor was there but no Freyja) father sent Gertrude and Bridget off with mother to take the shorter route home. We ambled down the banks of the stream called the Don where we would turn upstream when it reached the confluence of the Tyne. I broached the subject tentatively with my father, who I knew was preoccupied with the absence of Freyja at the Ascension service.

He grew increasingly attentive though, as I recounted my encounter with the mysterious stranger at the well and on Inner Farne. When I reached the conclusion of my story my father stood still in his tracks and, for the first time since Odin's disappearance, a broad grin broke across his face.

'You know what this means Bede don't you?" he asked, "You are destined for something special. God has chosen to make a special visitation. This is the best news I have received for ages. It has restored my faith in God." I could see he was filled with a renewed purpose and I could sense his mind whirring as he continued. "We must use the next few days in preparation my son. Let me think and I will come up with a plan." He could see a little pained expression cross my face and, like he had done so for so many times, he read my mind. "Don't worry son, there will be plenty of time for your kickbladder practice." I smiled with relief as we both sat on the bank reflecting on my revelation.

Father bent down and rummaged through the shale on the river bank, carefully selecting flat smooth pieces and discarding those stones which did not fit this category. I instinctively knew that this was the prelude to a water skimming competition which I also knew that I would come a poor second to my father.

We had played this many times and the most skims I had achieved was six. Father's record was a mammoth ten and I could see my news had reinvigorated him and motivated him to attempt to break his best score. He groaned as he straightened to an upright position in readiness of the forthcoming encounter. He then went to a half bent stance as he propelled the first stone, attempting to get it as horizontal as possible. I counted as it skipped - six, seven.......eight times.

"Wow! Well done dad, a great first attempt." My father grimaced as if to imply that he could do much better.

"I am a little out of practice son. It is a while since we've done this. Too long!" he smiled in reply, "Now it's your turn boy."

I cranked my arm back but could only manage five skims. Father warmed up with a further eight, followed by a nine whilst I could only match my five. I could see that Father was building up to one exceptional attempt but I did not realise just how exceptional it was going to be. He seemed lost in the activity, with all his cares and troubles banished. He bent low and thrust the object across the water.

As if in slow motion we watched in awe, as it skimmed easily the first half dozen steps. Then seven, eight, nine and then the record equalling ten, then a new record breaking eleventh skim. We both raised our arms in triumph as the stone attempted a further twelve skim. However the further record bid was thwarted as the projectile thwacked against the bow of a craft making its way up the river. We had been too engrossed in our activity to notice how the vessel had made its progress from the mouth of the river and was now negotiating a possible landing on the embankment near us.

We both raised our heads in query as we wondered who had dared to interrupt our world record skimming attempt. We saw a light wooden vessel approximately twenty feet long. In the stern sat a grey haired elderly gentleman, with matching beard, holding the arm of the tiller, carefully steering the boat to its safe harbour. In the middle of the vessel sat a woman of similar age who reflected a beautiful countenance for a lady of advancing years. She was anxiously transmitting instructions to her partner in the stern as they manoeuvred to their destination.

There sitting motionless in the bow of the boat was a young boy. He was serene and proud as he pointed to the shore. The stones which father and I were holding fell from our hands as we recognised the now grinning face of Odin.

Chapter Fifteen

Pentecost

The bright easterly rays of the sun burst through the cracks in the wooden shutter on the windows of the room I shared with my sister and younger brother. The branches of the tree five yards away made the light flicker in the gentle breeze. We were blessed as we had two bedrooms, one for us children and one for my parents. Most of my friends had only a one roomed house but we had three; two bedrooms and a living, kitchen room. My father called this open plan living but he insisted in creating our separate sleeping rooms.

I lay on my bed thinking about recent events and the day to come. I am sure you can imagine the excitement caused by Odin's return, with the two mysterious adults who turned out to be his mother's parents, his grandparents. The details of Odin's adventures in Scandinavia are for another day. But, after many trials and tribulations, he managed to locate his grandparents with the help of his captors! They then decided to embark on the hazardous journey across the North Sea to seek their long lost family. Odin's mother can hardly contain her joy at the return of her son and the added bonus of her parents arrival has also served to repair her relationship with my father. He is like a new man and has recaptured the playfulness which understandably deserted him when Odin was taken.

There was a quiet tap on the door and without a sound I assented to my father's silent command. I washed in the Heb Burn, knowing that I would soon trace its source to the well where I had a special rendezvous. I toileted nearby where father had constructed a private wooden box.

Excrement and urine would be flushed down a ceramic pipe using water from a bucket which stood next to the seat. The person using the toilet was then responsible for refilling the bucket. The pipe extended quite far into the river where it would catch the ebb and flow of the tide and eventually dissipate into the sea. Father credited this invention to the Romans who he had quite a respect for.

'This is a great day son. Pentecost! The birthday of the Christian church," he said with an air of excitement and anticipation.

I always thought it a bit odd that the church should have a birthday, nevertheless I recalled in detail the story my father had told me so often.

Pentecost was a harvest festival for the Jewish people and the feast was celebrated fifty days after Passover, which is just before Easter. Thousands of Jews from all over the world came to Jerusalem for the feast and a babble of languages could be heard in the streets. Jesus' friends gathered together, probably in a room within the Temple courts. It was nine o'clock in the morning, the public hour of prayer. They had gathered together fearful of any backlash there may be from the authorities now that they had discovered the body of Jesus had disappeared.

Suddenly there seemed to come from above the building a noise like a fierce wind rushing through the room. Above them, hovering under the ceiling, gleamed what looked like a mass of fire; and, as they watched, it separated into individual flames which floated through the air and flickered over the head of every disciple present.

They felt, flowing through them, a tremendous power and ecstasy unlike anything they had known before. One or two of them began to speak, but in languages they did not know. More and more joined in until all the disciples were shouting praise to God in foreign languages at the top of their voices; some laughing, some weeping with emotion and exaltation, as they felt themselves seized and uplifted by the enormous power of the Holy Spirit sweeping through them.

Round the building where they had met, crowds gathered quickly, wondering what the commotion could be. The disciples poured out into the open air, still shouting praise to God so that they could be heard throughout the Temple courts. Quickly little knots of people surrounded individual disciples. Here one talked Persian, another spoke beautifully in Greek; a third praised God in Arabic; a fourth sang a Coptic psalm.

The crowd was dumbfounded. "These are Galileans who can barely speak their own language properly. How is it that one of us hears them praising God so beautifully in our native tongues?" Some of the onlookers who heard the shouting and saw the disciples laughing and weeping with ecstasy said contemptuously, "They're drunk!"

But Peter heard them and when the noise had quietened a little, he called the other apostles to him and together they faced the crowd. No longer fearful Peter's voice rang out with confidence,

"Fellow Jews we are not drunk for it is still early in the day. No! What you have seen and heard is a fulfilment of the prophet Joel who prophesied a great outpouring of the Holy Spirit in the last days. Everyone then who calls on God will be saved. You all know of Jesus of Nazareth who worked miracles and signs among you. It was you who gave Him up to the heathen men to be crucified. However this was God's will, for He raised Jesus from the dead as He said He would. I know this to be true as I have seen Him with my own eyes. Jesus said He would give the Holy Spirit to all his believers and this is what you have seen this morning. Jesus is Lord and the Messiah."

The Jews were filled with remorse at what Peter had told them and asked what should they do. Peter said, "Turn away from your sins and be baptised in the name of Jesus and then you too will receive the Holy Spirit."

The people did repent of their sins and that day three thousand hearers became followers of Jesus.

My reverie was interrupted by father waving me to join him for the half mile walk along the banks of the burn to the well. When we arrived at the burn father confirmed what I had suspected; that today was to be the day of my baptism.

"Usually my son, people are not baptised into our faith until they are adults. But Godric and Bishop Benedict have recognised your readiness. I think your own experiences too have confirmed this."

"Yes father I am ready but will I feel drunk, like the apostles on that first Pentecost day?"

"They were drunk - with joy, not alcohol. You may feel like them or you may not. It is not about feelings son. Your feelings can change with the wind. No my boy, it is about faith. You must believe that your sins are forgiven by the waters of baptism and then you must believe that you are empowered by the baptism of the Spirit. Then you must draw on the power given to you this day, everyday of your life!"

Father then took me into a deep pool where the well drained into the burn. Stones beneath the waterline formed natural steps until the water covered over my waist. Father held my shoulders as he prayed,

"Bede! I baptise you in the name of the Father and of the Son and of the Holy Spirit." With that he dunked me bodily underneath the water for five seconds. As I splurged water he continued, "You have been crucified with Christ and by this baptism you have been cleansed from sin. You no longer live but it is Christ who lives in you." Then, laying his hands upon my head he said, "Bede, you are a new creation. In the name of Jesus Christ, receive the Holy Spirit and go preach His word to all nations."

The water dripped down my head and down my tunic as I stood in the cold water. My father now assumed the role of a minor participant in this holy event. I expected fireworks, like the first apostles or at least flashing lights like the Aurora Borialas or even an appearance from the mysterious stranger.

But no, all I felt was a serene calmness and a total reassurance that I had been ransomed, healed, restored and forgiven. I felt as light as a feather and as fearless as a lion. I knew that, from this day on, things would never be quite the same again.

Chapter Sixteen

The kickbladder Cup

Thankfully the fine late spring weather looks like it's going to last, as we sit on the embankment of the old Roman fort of Arbeia, looking over the mouth of the River Tyne at South Shields. The Romans had long since vacated this fort and its sister across the water at Segadunum. The buildings had fallen into ruin but there was a huge expanse of grass where the soldiers would have done their drills.

All the teams are assembled as we listen to the organiser going over the rules and regulations of the competition. We are quite familiar with them already as Agatha had attended a meeting of team managers (she was the only woman manager) and she in turn had held a meeting with our team to pass on the information. Yawns are being stifled as the speaker seems to like the sound of his own voice, and he waves his hands to emphasise the more important points. He is standing on the plinth of a column, with the remains of the actual column forming a natural dais for him to lean on. The decapitated stone head of some worthy Roman nobleman lies unceremoniously a few yards away. Once sitting on top of the column it now sits forlornly and forgotten, caressed by overgrown grass and weeds. I drag my attention away from my day dream about the former soldier to take in the finer points of the competition.

There are twelve teams which will be divided into four groups of three. The winners of each group will go forward to a semi final of four teams on a knockout basis, with the final following. Teams have come from Monkwearmouth and across the river at Wall's End as well as round about. There are two pitches marked out, each with the same sized goals. An official, called a referee, will take charge of the game and their decision is to be final and respected by all. They will attract our attention by blowing on a piece of reed. They tell us that only fair tackles will be allowed and free kicks will be awarded against transgressors. Matches are to last fifteen minutes each half. At half-time we turn around and kick the other way.

We had only decided at the last minute on the name of our team. As most of the team lived on or near the Heb stream we decided on the title of Heb Burn Celtic. We were going to be one of two teams from the area, the other being from nearby Jarrow. Controversially they had decided to call themselves Jarrow Vikings. Their name was announced to a chorus of boos! Family and friends had gathered to swell the numbers watching as we broke up to get some last minute directions from Agatha.

'Right girls and boys remember what we have worked on," she said. The game is about passing not just clogging the bladder up field. Keep it simple, when we have got the bladder support the person on the bladder. Give them options." Seeing our confusion she explained, "Make sure they have a choice of who to pass to. When we lose it get behind the bladder and make life difficult for your opponents. Remember! Don't tackle from behind and try to stay on your feet."

Agatha really knew what she was talking about and we would have done anything for her. However the first two games in the group stage did not go exactly to plan and it was only thanks to Joseph that we managed to scrape a one all draw in the first game. He popped up with a late equaliser to save our blushes. A second goalless draw followed but we had more success in our final group game. We still were not playing well but thanks to a Joseph hat trick, we won by the odd goal in five in the third game.

This meant that we finished on equal points with Tynemouth Priory. Only because we had scored more goals than them did we progress to the semi final stage. So we had a double debt of gratitude to Joseph; a point not lost on Agatha.

"Well if it wasn't for Joseph we would all be going home by now. He is the only one who has listened to my instructions." Joseph preened himself and was full of pride at our manager's comments. "Caedmon, you're supposed to be captain, yet I haven't heard you talking to the team. Bede you seem to have your head in the clouds and girls..." she glared at Helen and Jane, "You can do a lot better. I have given you a big build up and you have let me down." None of us had ever seen this side of Agatha and everybody noticeably braced themselves for more. "I suggest that Odin and the rest of the reserves get themselves ready to come on in the next game." With a final flourish she waved us away in disgust.

Her words had an immediate effect as Caedmon assumed full control as captain and underpinned Agatha's comments with his own more earthy rallying call. We all were more determined, Eldrick his brother even more so, in our approach to what hopefully, would be our penultimate game.

Our opponents in the semi final are the most feared team in the competition; Wall's End. Feared because they seemed to be the biggest team (both girls and boys) in the competition. Feared also because they were from an area of Northumbria which had the reputation for being one of the roughest. Wall's End was a settlement at the eastern end of a huge wall built by the Roman Emperor Hadrian. It was built to keep unruly Scotsmen at bay but one look at the residents that faced us today, would be enough to send anyone packing.

We looked from one to another and the same idea occurred subliminally to us all. This game could not be won physically but through skill alone. Agatha's advice to pass the bladder would be crucial and we realised that we must not give possession away cheaply. This determination was sufficient to see us through to half time without any score and we could see that our opponents were becoming increasingly frustrated. This frustration boiled over in the second half when they targeted our star player Joseph, bringing him down as he was just about to score. The referee signalled a penalty which Caedmon dispatched coolly into the left corner of the goal. Truly a captain's goal and he signalled to us all to settle down.

Unfortunately Joseph had been hurt in the encounter and could not continue. This was devastating news, as our main threat had been nullified, albeit at the expense, to our opponents, of a goal. However Agatha pulled of a master stroke of tactics when she brought on Odin as substitute. What we needed was someone who could hold on to the bladder and, with Odin's dribbling skills, we had that person. So, with him running down the sand timer and us surviving some scares at the back we managed to see the game out and found ourselves in the final.

Agatha came bounding over with a grin as wide as the mouth of the Tyne below us. She hugged Odin and Joseph telling them that we owed so much to them. Joseph flushed with embarrassment then hobbled away and it was obvious to us all that he was not going to be fit for the final. His embarrassment turned to tears when he realised the situation. Helen put a comforting arm around him and Agatha ordered treatment with ice, which she had been keeping in an old Roman ice room in the ruins of the fort. She had thought of everything and the swelling around Joseph's calf subsided noticeably.

"I still don't think that you will be fit enough to start the game but I may be able to bring you on later in the final," said Agatha, which mollified Joseph and his tears abated. "Right you all need to take on water and rest as we have some time whilst they play the second semi final. The final will not start for another hour yet."

An hour or so later we lined up for the first ever Northumbria Kickbladder Cup Final against our arch rivals Jarrow Vikings, who had come through by hammering Sunter Land four nothing. We knew many of their players, having played against them locally and their top player, Chloe, was receiving rave reports; as much as our top player Joseph. We certainly had our work cut out if we were to lift the trophy without our star performer. It was to be a match of the stripes too. Our red and white tunics against their black and white tunics. Ironically in the first half we played the best kickbladder we had played all tournament, yet found ourselves three goals down at half time thanks to a brilliant Chloe hat trick. Agatha changed things at half time with two of our girls marking Chloe out of the game in the second half. Eldrick managed to pull one back with a header from a brilliant cross from yours truly. In one last throw of the dice, Joseph came on as sub and immediately set up Odin for number two. Phew! Joseph megged the keeper for an injury time equaliser which took us into extra time.

The golden goal rule meant that, the next team to score would win the tournament. This looked like it would be the Vikings as Chloe squandered an excellent opportunity. This proved costly as Jane jinked up the wing, cut inside and rolled the ball under the keeper and into an empty net. Our supporters went wild, as Jane was mobbed by her teammates. Agatha waved us to recognise our opponents and shake their hands, then she too shook hands with her counterpart, then came over and congratulated us.

Our master of ceremonies who had instructed us at the beginning of the tournament, told us that Bishop Benet himself would be presenting the trophy. We all lined up and he shook us all by the hand before he presented Caedmon with the large pewter cup, which he held aloft. We then ran around the pitch on a lap of honour. I arrived back to see my father deep in conversation with Bishop Benet.

"Ah Bede, well done," said the youthful looking bishop. We had all heard stories about his many travels round the world. "I was just discussing with you father an idea I have had. I will let him tell you but I look forward to seeing you tomorrow." With that he swept off with his entourage of monks, presumably to St. Paul's monastery, Jarrow where, I inferred, I would be seeing him tomorrow.

As I walked home with father I looked at him imploringly for an explanation. His silence perturbed me and it was not until our home was in sight, that he stopped and invited me to sit with him on a nearby rock overlooking the burn.

"You know son that your aunt and uncle will be joining us soon for her confinement." he began as I nodded my agreement, "I am afraid your room will be needed." He could see from my puzzled expression that I was wondering where I was going to be accommodated. "Bishop Benet has suggested that you might like to stay at the monastery." He raised his eyebrows in an attitude of questioning, expecting my obedient assent. As we stood up to complete our homeward journey he had one further enigmatic comment. "Bishop Benet will have more to say to you tomorrow. But remember my boy you will always be our son and your heart will always be in Heb Burn."

Chapter Seventeen

From the bes to the Don

I said farewell to my family today and walked the two miles to St. Paul's on my own with the few belongings I posses; a change of tunic and undergarment, a reed whistle, my trusty sling shot, a small knife and a water skin. I had a strange foreboding as my mother hugged and kissed me and father shook me by the hand and embraced me. My mother also thrust some bread and cheese into my hand and told me to make sure I was well looked after. I got the distinct feeling that I was leaving for longer than the period of my aunt's pregnancy. Nevertheless I did not feel inclined to query my parents and stoically told them not to worry as I would be fine.

I kept to the familiar river bank path, in order to avoid any possible inquisitors, as I did not wish to have to justify my actions until I was in full possession of the facts. The monastery was set in perfect isolation overlooking the river, with the Don stream burbling past the building.

I was met by Father Prior who showed me to a monk's cell with a small square window framing the stream's confluence with the larger river. A table and chair was squeezed in against one wall, with a sturdy wooden bed against the opposite wall, covered with a thick hessian blanket. The only decoration was a carved oak cross, hanging as a reminder of our

Saviour's sacrifice. Father Prior asked me to make myself comfortable and that he would send someone for me in an hour. He obviously did not realise my meagre belongings meant that I would be settled in, well within that time.

I sat at the table come writing desk and wondered about who the previous inhabitant of the cell had been. When full, the monastery could accommodate sixty monks but there was about forty or so at the Jarrow community now and a further three hundred or so at the sister house at Monkwearmouth on the River Wear. Plans were afoot to increase the accommodation at Jarrow as vocations were increasing. There was a fair amount of movement by monks between the two communities with the Wearside monastery housing the communities' leader Benet Biscop, also known as Bishop Benet or Bishop Benedict. It was the distinguished bishop himself who soon sent for me.

I was taken to the monastery library by a young novice monk hardly any older than me, perhaps sixteen or seventeen summers. All the way through the labyrinth of corridors, which led to the Abbot's room, the novice remained taciturn. Clad in Benedictine black, with the cowl of his habit pulled forward, he looked menacing. When we reached the room I was greeted by the man I had met for the first time when he had presented us yesterday with the trophy.

"Bede my boy welcome to our community. You must be very proud of your achievement." As he sat me down he nodded a dismissal to the young novice monk and proceeded to discuss at some length and with some knowledge, the previous day's events. He told me that he too had played a form of kickbladder himself when growing up but without the formal rules of yesterday's competition. I politely conversed with him but I could see he sensed my disquiet at my real presence here. Clearing his throat he signalled a change of subject.

"Now then Bede you must be wondering why you are here. I think you realise that it is about more than providing respite care, whilst your Aunt has her baby." He paused "You see Bede you're not the only one who has had an encounter with a mysterious stranger. When you pray to God, He hears and he answers. As a community we have been praying. We have entered into the presence of God; the Holy of Holies. God has revealed that He has a special plan for you. A plan for good, a plan to further His kingdom here on earth."

He paused again and seeing that his words were finding a home in my heart he continued.

"Bede you must discover what God has planned for you. You must discover your vocation. Your father agrees you can stay here, if you wish, and seek the will of God for your life."

I could only show my agreement by my silence. Jesus said that we must take up our cross, deny ourselves and follow him. He tells us that those who try to hang on to their lives will lose it and those who lose their lives for His sake, will find it. I just knew that if I gave up my life at Heb Burn then I would find it. Father Abbot continued,

"Bede we want you to stay here and explore your calling. It does not mean that you will not see your family or your friends. You can see your mam and dad whenever you like. Your friends will still come here to school. You will play with them and grow with them. But you will do more schooling. You will study the Bible, the history of the world and science. You will travel and meet people, you will be used of God. Go back to your cell and contemplate all I have said. If you are not happy. be assured you are free to go. Be assured too you are always free to come and go."

I traced my way back to my cell without the aid of anyone. I arrived at my new accommodation and felt a sense of home. Since my baptism and confirmation on that Pentecost day I had felt different. I had always felt as if I were an observer in life; on the outside looking in. Since that day I have felt part of life, part of being human, part of the great community of love. I knew now that I was destined for great things. I am not being big headed because they are great things that God has already planned for me to do and it is only through His power, that I will be enabled. I knew I had to deny the Heb Burn, deny my family, deny my dad. Lose my life, yet find it.

I instinctively fell to my knees in front of the carved simple cross on the wall and praised God for his greatness.

The Prayer

Christ Our Morning Star

By

Bede The Venerable

O Christ, our Morning Star
Splendour of light Eternal
Shining with the glory of the rainbow,
Come and waken us
From the greyness of our apathy,
And renew in us you gift of hope.

Books By The Author

Bede's Well – The Bede Trilogy
A Novel About The Boyhood of the Venerable Bede

Bede's World – The Bede Trilogy
A Novel About The Youth of the Venerable Bede

Bede's Way – The Bede Trilogy
A Novel About The Manhood of the Venerable Bede

A Man After My Own Heart
A Novel About King David

Insurable Interest
A Novel Set in The Financial Sector

15 Minute Short Stories
Rite of Passage Short Stories

Details of Other Publications
www.joestewart.weebly.com

Printed in Poland
by Amazon Fulfillment
Poland Sp. z o.o., Wrocław